# THE ALMOST-WEDDING OF JOHN BARRON GREY

## AMONG THE MYTHOS BOOK 5

RUTHANNE REID

# CONTENTS

## Copyright

Copyright © 2024 by **Ruthanne Reid**

All rights reserved. No part of this publication may be reproduced, distributed or transmitted in any form or by any means, without prior written permission.

**NO AI TRAINING:** Without in any way limiting the author's exclusive rights under copyright, any use of this publication to "train" generative artificial intelligence (AI) technologies to generate text is expressly prohibited. The author reserves all rights to license uses of this work for generative AI training and development of machine learning language models.

**www.ruthannereid.com**

Publisher's Note: This is a work of fiction. Names, characters, places, and incidents are a product of the author's imagination. Locales and public names are sometimes used for atmospheric purposes. Any resemblance to actual people, living or dead, or to businesses, companies, events, institutions, or locales is completely coincidental.

**The Almost-Wedding of John Barron Grey/ Ruthanne Reid**. – 1st ed.

# ⊀ HUMAN AUTHORED

Reg #: 3481501, https://authorsguild.org/human

Formatted using Lacuna

"Only those who will risk going too far can possibly find out how far it is possible to go."

——T.S. Eliot

# CHAPTER 1

## HARDBALL

Really, why would a Fey person ever *need* to rob a bank?

It doesn't add up. John Barron Grey, *né* McCarrig, is not the kind of guy to casually blow up his life. He's no Feyling; this guy's heir to the damn Throne, and he's been running around Earth decidedly uncrowned and uncaught for a couple hundred years. Someone that smart wouldn't do something like this.

Well, he went and did it anyway, and got himself arrested, babbling the whole time about *knowing his rights* and *wanting his investigator* and mugging for every camera he could find until he became an online sensation.

Even if they wanted to bury him, they couldn't after that. Just the kind of cause that gets people riled: sporting a purple bruise on one lovely cheek, his pouty lips defiant. Startling silver-blue peepers and long, thin ears drooping pitifully past his shoulders, trembling and pink. Ridiculous. Also enough to con the unsuspecting public onto his side, and there are protests.

Why, though? Why'd he do this? That question is probably never gonna be answered for me, and it's already driving me nuts.

Then, about two in the morning, my rival sends me one of the videos of this guy along with the warning, *This guy is gonna ask for one of us.*

Scott was right. The runaway prince's desire for an investigator leads him right to my door.

Fantastic. Because getting tangled up with the *gods-damned Throne* is exactly what I want to do on a Saturday morning.

At least I'll get some answers.

"Thank you for seeing me, detective," he says, gorgeous eyes wide, absolutely all-in with his *poor-me* schtick, and flips his silvery hair over his shoulder, though the effect is dimmed somewhat by the heavy iron bracelets they got him in.

"Real stylish," I say, pointing at the cuffs. "They make you wear those all night?"

"Oh, they *did*, detective," he says, holding them up like exhibit one. "It's been *terrible*, cut off from my magic like this."

I sigh. Human law enforcement *still* believes in nonsense like cold iron, and forgets which part of the Fey body does the conjuring. It ain't the hands. "Sure," I say.

"Unconscionable," he says, eyes lidded, and with flawless sleight of hand, deposits the still-closed cuffs on my desk.

Mm. Don't like *that*. "This needs coffee. Want a cup?"

He bats his eyelashes again like he didn't just flaunt the law at me. "Please."

It's not really a weird choice for him to pick investigation instead of ordinary legal defense. Since magic got revealed to the human world in a freak accident of draconic ascension and civil war, it's been a lot of adjustments for everybody, and this is one of them: if you're charged with a crime involving magical shit, you can do a lawyer *or* an investigator, because human lawyers tend to be a little too siloed to provide a good defense, whereas us good old gumshoes can track mud anywhere.

Still. I got a lot of questions why a renegade Fey prince is sitting in my grungy office. "So, Mr. McCarrig," I start.

"Just Grey," he says.

Huh. So that rumor's confirmed.

I eye him. "You sure? I don't give a dick about politics in here, but even I know that's an insult." Only Fey cut off from the Throne and Scepter, banished to potential death, are given that title.

His smile is one I reluctantly like: a little too bitter to be pretty, but strong, real, sure. "I made it a mark of pride."

Good for him, if true. "Whatever floats your boat." I hand him his coffee.

He takes it, and then he sings. Just a hum, really. Barely a *la*. Instantly, his black coffee lightens, and whipped cream rises from its depths like some reverse glacier.

Fey. I swear. I can sing fine, but my voice don't do *that*. "You could've asked for cream."

"*You* could've called for help," he says with a glance at the useless cuffs.

What, it was a fucking test? "You aren't been that scary yet," I say.

He laughs like silver bells. "Flatterer." He throws back the coffee, gulping it fast, then licks the whipped cream off his upper lip as part of the show.

I slow-clap. "So. Grey. I can't help being curious why you came to me instead of Scott. He's more your class."

After all, there's only two licensed Kin gumshoes in this town: me and Nate Scott. Scott's the classy one. I'm the guy who smashes plates.

"Oh," Grey says with a light, quick tone he hasn't used before. "That's easy. *You* barter. Famously, yeah? Nathanial Scott doesn't."

It's true my rival dearest doesn't barter. It's cold hard digital cash for him, or nothing. "True. Though it's not Nathanial. It's Natural. Nate's short for Natural."

Grey blinks. "How unusual! Poor thing was probably bullied."

"Yeah, I'm sure he had a real rough childhood chewin' on that silver spoon," I drawl. "So why don't you tell me what the hell brings you in here?"

And back to the big eyes, pitiful and pleading. "I might be here under slightly disingenuous circumstances."

Uh-huh.

I'm sure my reaction betrays my interest. I can keep my breath nice and steady, but I know my pupils dilate. He's offering me the biggie: information. "All right. And you're gonna explain the whole thing to me now, right?"

He actually *sniffles,* pleading and helpless and pretty. "You see, detective... I don't need to be exonerated."

Oh, boy. "Yeah? You like prison?"

"Not exactly, but it's better than the alternative. I need to stay there for a while."

"Why?"

He looks utterly ashamed of himself. "Because the Throne wishes to make me marry and produce an heir since I'm, you know, off being distinctly un-heir-like. I won't do it. So I need to stay out of reach until she changes her mind, and imprisonment is one way to do that."

I lean back in my creaky chair and study the guy.

Having confessed, Grey watches me back without so much as a guilty twitch. His ears go relaxed, up and slightly out, forming a happy little *V* of Fey body-language saying, *Hey, come closer, I've got no bat to swing.*

No; no, this sounds too easy. Fey logic broke Occam's razor years ago and used the shards to make half-truths shiny. He's running more than one game. "I don't know that I buy that, Grey."

Big eyes, absolutely guileless. "It's all true," he says.

"I'm sure it is, but it doesn't quite fill in all the gaps, does it?"

His smile fades.

I count off on my fingers. "Why ask for investigation at all? You could stay in the system without anybody's help. Just piss off the judge."

He wrinkles his nose. "And risk them figuring out I'm *trying* to stay locked up? I'd be extradited at once."

Hm. Maybe. "Sure. Why not a lawyer, then? They glue up the works, especially when paid by the hour. You came to a guy who gets things done, and that seems to be the opposite of what you're asking for here."

"If I don't seek counsel of *some* kind, I risk them realizing I don't want to get out—and a lawyer would never help me do this, anyway."

I scoff. "But you think I would?"

"Well, yes. Your reputation isn't just for getting things done, Mr. Night. It's also for helping those in need."

"I help real problems. I ain't so sure this *is* one. Can't you just say no? It's not like you haven't been defying the Throne openly for centuries."

His eyes lid. It's a smart look, wicked sharp, distinctly unlike the whole spoiled-prince shtick. "You researched me?"

"Agreed to see you, didn't I?"

"The Throne is impossible to say no to in person," he mumbles.

I give him *the look.* "Except you did already when you walked out. What's your real game here?"

"I need to stay in jail."

Nope. Denied. Buzzer sound. "That's *part* of the truth," I say, starting a mental list of *shit the pretty Fey won't answer.* "See, the problem with a case like *yours* is it's going to drag out."

His eyes are pleading. "Isn't that the point?"

"Three problems with that. One, you don't actually need me, so this is a waste of both our time. You've been around long enough. You absolutely already know how to stay in prison without help."

"Oh, well," he starts, but I'm not finished.

"Two is Scott. He's got a chip on his shoulder. Gets competitive. Does things like float a bet with his one serious rival about finishing a certain number of cases before the end of the year."

He goes stiff. "You took that bet?"

"I did. I know our styles; nobody's cutting corners to win. Problem is, your case has no end *by design*, and it might be enough busywork to keep me from taking on more clients."

"It's barely a *case*. How could it take up that much time?" he grouses, his ears angled back and down.

Because of how I work, but I'm on a roll now. "Three, the Throne has extradition, though she almost never uses it. She can just demand you back whenever she wants, and you can't tell me you didn't factor that in."

I caught him. "Ah-ha," he says, drooping.

"Yeah. So right now, I'm not seeing a good reason to take you on. You don't need me. You need a slow-as-molasses lawyer, or your own shenanigans."

"Shenanigans! Oh, Mr. Night," He tilts his head, and the pitiful look drops. "You have another reputation, too—of a very annoying tendency to uncover things your clients didn't necessarily want found."

That's it. That's why he's here.

Because I *do* that. I'm good at this, real good, and my clients learn fast that hiding shit from me don't work out so well. "And what is it you hope I'll stumble into, Grey?"

His ears twitch. "Politics?" he suggests. "Really, I'm just hoping you make a big enough mess to keep all eyes on you."

It's beginning to feel he's dug a giant trap, hid it under a giant rug, and dangled bait over the middle. "Try again."

"You know, if you're not interested, I'll just consult with Scott after all," he says, deflecting.

"He won't take you." I tap my jaw. "Heard the whole thing. It's me or nothing, and *nothing* is extradition."

*Aw, come on, Night, he'd make a great chew toy,* says Scott through my implant.

Grey gasps like a poet, pressing his hands to his heart. "You've had him listening the whole time?"

Ha. "You already guessed he was."

He laughs and leans forward, cupping his face, elbows on his knees, and he looks like some work of art, some absolute pixie-ass dream, beautiful to behold, his daggers hidden deep. "Unfortunately, Simon Night, I'm afraid I *can't* answer your questions."

Okay, then. It's time to play hardball.

The drama of this is how I'm gonna catch him. Yeah, I want this weird case, want to know what's going on, but it has to be on my terms, not his. Threats will get nowhere. So instead, it's time for abandonment.

"Then I don't have a new client." I stand.

"What?" he says, ears going straight back like exclamation points.

"Guess all those viewers are gonna be real disappointed."

"Wait, we're done?" he says like a guy who was just getting warmed up.

"Sorry. The bait's good, I'll give you that, but it just ain't juicy enough for me. Best of luck with the wedding." I open the door.

Grey looks between it and me, where the cops are waiting out there, shooting the shit and sipping my coffee, waiting to take him back to prison *without* an investigator. They can't see us—my own wards are still up—but the point still comes across.

"Wait," he says.

I don't close the door. "Off you go," I say.

He breaks faster than I expected him to. "It involves the Raven King!" he blurts, then hunches down in his seat, ears low, eyes huge.

My blood goes cold, and given my heritage, that's saying something. I close the door.

*What?* says Scott in my ear. *What did he say?*

I sit back down.

Grey's looking like he has some *regrets*. "Forget I said that."

*Night. Walk away now.*

"Whoa." I hold up my hand, and it doesn't even shake. "Whoa, whoa. What? The Raven King? The fucking *Lord of Umbra?* You're shitting me."

He shakes his head no. "Not shitting you."

*Night. Don't be stupid about this.*

I ignore Scott. "You're telling the truth?"

"Yes?"

"How is he involved?"

"I can't tell you," Grey whines. "I shouldn't even have said that much. I panicked, all right?"

That's a hell of a bait he's hung over that rug.

With perfect timing, a ghostly countdown appears in my peripheral—my A.I. politely letting me know I have five minutes left of consult time.

They're waiting right now to take him back to prison. If I turn him down, Scott really won't take him on—he won't touch anything involving Celestial powers—and there straight-up isn't anyone else in the city qualified for whatever the fuck this is.

I gotta know. I gotta. Carrot, stick. Damn.

*Don't do it, Night,* Scott warns.

Grey looks penitent. His ears are up and forward, perky, but they're trembling; that means he's fighting the reflex for them to go down and back, tucked out of the way, like a scared little cat.

*Don't do it,* Scott says again. *You'll lose our bet.*

I have to do it. I have to know. "I'll do it," I say, and Scott goes silent. Now that Grey's my client, confidentiality is triggered, and he'll be out of the loop. "Cassilda, tell Sargeant Burl I'm accepting the case. They'll need to set up communication and visits, and give me more time now."

*Got it,* says my artificial assistant.

Grey sags, and it doesn't take a pro to see relief in every inch of his Fey self.

# CHAPTER 2

## PLAYING ALONG

Turns out it wouldn't have mattered if Scott stayed on the line. Grey isn't the most difficult client I've had, but he's up there.

Can't or won't tell me more. I question him for half an hour, and I get *nothing* out of the guy. "I really am sorry," he says apologetically. "I had to take some very tricky oaths to get as far as I did. I'm trying to answer you."

He is, but magical oaths are binding. There's little either of us can do about it.

Fey and their *complications*. They didn't break Occam's razor. They ground it into dust and gave it to passersby, hidden in the booze. "Give me something, damn you," I say.

"I did, and I'm probably going to be in trouble for it," he says.

Shit. "Are you in danger? The Raven King coming after you?" I say, low. "If you need protection, I know some folks."

He gives me a look of surprise, and then warmth, like he hadn't expected the offer. "Not that kind of trouble. He's just going to be put out for a few days. He's not going to hurt me."

The Raven King's reputation says otherwise. "My offer stands. Look, we're out of time. I'm gonna dig into this. I may find shit you don't want found."

"As long as you make some noise so everyone thinks things are happening while I stay in prison, knock yourself out," he says, which really does seem to be his goal.

Well, I warned him. "Suit yourself."

"I'm *trying* to do just that," he huffs just as they come a-knocking, ready to drag him back outside.

As he goes, the actor in him switches on. He looks exactly like he should for anybody watching: beat down but hopeful, vulnerable but brave. A beautiful target for a social media frenzy.

He's leaving me with a mystery, and precisely three directions I can look for clues: the room Grey was renting; the bank he broke into; and word on the street, which might tell me why in *fuck* the Raven King would be involved.

It doesn't make sense. What's in Boston that might ever interest him? He's got a whole parallel world, Umbra; he literally rules the People of the Darkness. Since sea levels rose last century, and elevated storms wrecked the coasts, Boston is tiny. Like, pre-Revolutionary War tiny. The Raven King has no damn reason to come here.

Although now I wonder if the answer might be in that bank.

Grey broke in, but as far as the report goes, he didn't actually take anything. He broke in—fucked with the locks, undid the wards—then sat in the middle of the floor and waited for them to arrest him. Weird. I wonder if the official report left out anything *inconvenient*.

Logic says to check the place Grey was living first. I could find some lingering etheric resonance, or someone who saw something, and the more time passes, the less of that there'll be... but I got a gut feeling about that bank.

Not for the first time, I wish I could be in two places at once. Unfortunately, in this town, I've only got one option if I want to cover all the roads. *Scott. Got a minute?*

*Your client gone?* he responds coolly.

*Yeah. You up for a sub-contract?*

A pause.

I fold my arms on the desk and rest my forehead on them. This'll go well.

*Bit off more than you can chew?* he says, still tetchy.

*Yes or no, Scott.*

*No. Just got a case myself, actually. Sorry, Night.*

So much for that. Stupid rival. *Thanks, anyway,* I grumble, and end the call.

Okay, bank or apartment? *Cassilda. Flip a coin.*

*On it, boss,* she says, and in my periphery, a ghostly coin appears, flashing as it flips through the air, landing perfectly on my desk with a realistic clink. Heads.

"Bank it is," I say, and go to grab my coat.

It's always cold here.

I'm okay with that. I've read about how bad the climate emergency got before the People of the Sun got involved—about the cyclonic storms, the hungry ocean eating islands and coasts, the endless droughts fucking over crops, the merciless temperatures wiping out entire species and killing more and more humans by the year.

Then the Sun stepped in, and saved their stupid asses.

The People of the Sun are all about *healing* and *stability* and all, but the fact is, they didn't have to offer it. Humans—the ones in charge—were not *asking* to be pulled out of the hole they'd dug. It was a life-raft given when none was expected.

I mean, Earth had an okay relationship with the other Peoples after the New Delhi Incident, when dragon ascension and infighting revealed magic to the world, but no one expected help for the whole planet.

I've read a lot of theories on just what happened when the People of the Sun approached the human governments with their solution. Nobody knows what was given in trade; nobody knows what agreements were made.

What we *do* know is that within thirty years, they'd calmed the atmosphere, soothed the rising waves, and began the slow turnaround toward a livable planet.

All this was before I was born, of course. I not only came around after the New Delhi Incident, but also after the place got cleaned up enough for business. Lucky me.

I still would like to know what the trade-off was, though. It took an incredible amount of power to make the changes they did, and it's not like now the Earth belongs to anyone but humans.

At least they learned their lesson. Human power these days comes from wind and solar, nano-tech, surveillance, etcetera. Good for them. I still prefer having magic, even if being Kin *does* make me a mutt.

I look up. It's New England to a T today, gray and bright, cool with a kiss of moisture, just enough so it might rain or it might mist or it might do nothing at all but fog up any glass that leaves warm homes.

Eh, better check. *Cassilda, am I gonna be rained on?*

*No rain predicted, boss,* says my faithful assistant.

Good. Don't want to waste any magic keeping dry.

The bank Grey picked isn't a big one, but that's not what makes it weird. I would've thought he'd pick an Ever-Dying bank. It's logical: he couldn't do one owned by the Sun, because they're legalists, and would turn him over to the Throne. The Darkness would just keep him; he'd make a nice snack. Fey obviously wouldn't work, and the Guardian and Dream have neither a world, nor banks.

Ever-Dying, they'd keep him the way he wants: in jail. A chance to get one over on a magical race? They'd do it in a heartbeat. But instead, Grey went for a Kin bank.

Kin are mixes. We have good relations with most other Peoples out of necessity for survival. He risked the Kin owners of this bank handing him back to the Throne. Why the heck did he pick a Kin bank? "This guy's gonna make me crazy," I mutter to myself.

*Need a pick-me-up, boss?* says Cassilda.

*Naw,* I think at her. *Just keep an eye out. Wanna do this low-key as possible.*

*Already on it, boss.*

This is why I won't swap her out for a newer model. Didn't even have to tell her to do that.

Of course, I'm under surveillance just for existing. There's magical surveillance and non-magical surveillance, and I got ways to beat both; have to, in my line of work. But it can be real suspicious if you're not careful about it. People still have eyes, and disappearing right off the street in front of them ain't a good look.

So while Cassilda keeps an eye out for tails, I focus on my plan: to whack this nest with a stick and see what falls out.

I'm visible as I turn on Fourth, coming in sight of the bank. Visible as I saunter to the cafe across the street from the place, facing all the subtle, high-class versions of *fuck off if you're illicit* signs. I'm visible as I get a coffee and sit in a chair, looking directly at the front doors.

A human guard stands there, paying less attention than he should; he's just for show, anyway. Old-fashioned shit to appease the bigots. The real security is studying me: artificial intelligence, having by now already identified me, and alerted whoever needs to know that I'm here.

They'll know I'm not here for no reason. Let's see what happens.

I sip my coffee. It's a pretty good latte; Silver Dawning-sourced milk still tastes better to me, no matter how good Earth cows are doing these days.

I'll give them about an hour to respond. If nothing happens by that point, I'll go in and see if they'll let me ask a few questions. They get cagey, I'll get a writ from a judge, and they'll have to answer me.

We'll see how they want this to go down.

Fifteen minutes later, three men in dark suits and sunglasses exit the bank and head across the street, not even pretending I'm not their target.

I stand, hand my empty mug back over the counter, straighten my tie, and wait for them.

The three of them are human, and quite large. It's probably meant to be intimidating. If I were human, it probably would be. "Mr. Night?" says the tallest one, who's two hundred centimeters at least.

"Present and accounted for," I say, leaning into my Bahstonian.

"Come this way, please," he says.

Is this what I wanted to happen? Sure, but I didn't expect it to be quite so shady. "If you tell me why."

These three goombas look at each other. "Your appointment," says the spokesperson.

My what?

Okay. We all know this is being recorded from a thousand angles. My response determines a lot, especially if they try to disappear me. To play along or not play along? "This a friendly visit? You willing to swear to that?"

"I wouldn't know, sir," says the guy.

Curiosity has always been my biggest weakness. Hell, I'd be "investigating" shit even if I had to have a *real* job. "All right. Sure. Let's go have an appointment."

All three of them look relieved, which warns me this manager can't be too kind a person; they were afraid of getting a *no*. Goodie. The spokesperson leads the way, but the other two flank me, like they think it's perfectly reasonable I might make a break for it, and just their job to prevent it.

No worries on that front. I *gotta* see what the fuss is about.

# CHAPTER 3

## MISTAKEN IDENTITY

*Eleanore Lin,* Cassilda informs me as I'm led into the lady's glassed-in office, though I already knew who this was the second I clapped eyes on her.

Of course the bank manager is a Lin. Good job, Night, you've jumped feet-first into something way bigger than you.

This is gonna be fun.

Lin, Blackwood, Lester, Sims, Doe, Yang, Bard, Roth, and Williams are the nine big name families among the People of the Kin.

Oh, there's loads of *families*; we're our own People, after all, one of the mighty seven silos into which everybody sapient gets dumped. But those nine? They matter. See, those nine are the ones who sued for and *got* that People status. Who fought for and won the right to take all us leftovers, us half-breeds, us something-human-something-else combinations that nobody wanted, and made us into a force to be respected.

We even made it onto the Great Wheel of the Seven Peoples of the Earth.

(See the branch? Yeah, that's the Kin. 'Cause we *branch off*. Nothing like a dad joke immortalized.)

There are nine leaves because *nine families*, and they're listed in order of importance. Look who's at the top! Lin.

They *led the charge*. They've got Myrddin, one of the most powerful beings alive. They're wealthy, and powerful, and hey, if the Lins bring accusations against a guy, nobody will take that guy's side, no matter what proof he has.

So, yeah. In over my head. But I think the bigger question is why in hell a Kin powerhouse wants to see *me*.

"Mr. Night," she says, unsmiling, and nods at the chair across her desk.

So funny, how we cling to these visual representations of organization and power. We barely need desks; everything can be completely digital, projected, or magical and straight-up depictive. But we like things we can touch, hold; we like the feel of a desk, of paper (albeit expensive and carefully sourced) with its special smell and texture, of symbols of authority and education and rights. So, sure, I sit across from her desk, and we both pretend the paper she's neatly stacked and the pens in her little cup mean anything to anyone but our primitive selves.

Eleanor Lin, one of the most influential beings in all four worlds, threads her fingers and looks at me like I tracked mud in her carpet. "You're not who I expected."

So is there an appointment or not? "Funny you thought it'd be that predictable," I say with every ounce of bullshit I've ever thrown at anyone.

"Our debt is finally paid," she says, and slides a small, brown-wrapped parcel across the desk.

What in hell?

So. Got two choices here. One: play along, pretend to be whoever she expected, and try to fake my way out with whatever this is. Two: fess up.

Two has all kinds of downsides, including this convo getting shut right the hell down. One has a lot *more* downsides. I have no guarantee this's got anything to do with me or Grey. I'm getting involved in something with a seriously powerful family, and could be painting a target on my head for no reason. I don't even know where to take this thing, but since they'll know I took it, I can be tracked down by them *and* the intended recipient.

Then there's this: somebody hired someone *enough like me* that she assumes I'm the stooge. My gut instinct says this does involve me, somehow.

All that aside... I gotta know. "Got any advice?" I say, not taking the package yet to see what she does.

She turns away, facing some pastoral landscape hung on the wall. "Nothing beyond the instructions already given."

That went nowhere.

More thoughts on this mess. One: after this, she'll be embarrassed, and definitely will not be answering any questions. Two: she's got to know Grey hired me; that was all over the news, so she knows I'm connected to him. Three: she still thinks I'm her guy, and that is fucking *intriguing.*

Four: I will spend the rest of my life kicking myself if I don't jump into this clusterfuck. I slide the package toward me. It's wrapped in old brown fake paper, flat, feather-light, and irregularly shaped. I don't have a clue what it is, but nobody looks spooked that I tuck it inside my jacket pocket, so it's not gonna kill me by proximity. "Good luck."

"Same to you," she says, hands folded in her lap, studying that painting like she'd give her right foot to be there instead of here.

Which tells me we *both* got targets on our heads.

I nod at her. Nod at the goons. Walk out, calm, not rushing, not running, though I can't keep my heart rate from picking up like it wants to dance the tango.

*Cassilda, I'm gonna be followed, I'm sure. Full alert.*

*Spousal permissions?*

*Restricted,* I say, because I don't want to drag anybody into this if I just got myself killed.

*You got it, boss,* she says, and in front of me and around me, barely visible, the layout of several blocks rises in three-dimensional glory like etchings on glass, showing me where people are as little blue dots, where cameras are as little green dots (everywhere), where vehicles are.

I turn right out of the bank, opposite of the way I came, and I don't miss that the goons watch me go like maybe they doubt Ms. Lin had the right idea.

So far, so good. Turn the corner. Past a little bakery, past an old, blue mailbox behind glass with a little plaque explaining what this thing used to be for. Past some trees transplanted from somewhere *not Earth,* their leaves glowing gently green even in the full light of day.

I need to disappear soon. Just gotta find a blind spot so there's no record of—

I get a call. The ID is... unexpected. *Scott?*

*Night,* says Nate Scott, and his usual upper-crust smooth has gone ragged. *Did you just fucking scoop my case?*

Ooooooh, boy.

Scott does not swear. Feel like I oughta buy him a drink over it. *Not on purpose, if I did,* I tell my rival, ducking into an alley, watching all those dots on Cassilda's projection. *Eleanor's got the blame for that.*

A moment of silence.

*He's activated tracking,* Cassilda says.

*Block him.*

*Already did, boss. You're on high alert.*

And here, I'd feared that would be going overboard. *You still there?*

*Night, you don't know what you're dealing with. Bring it back.*

Except whoever set this up did it in such a way that she expected a Kin detective, and there's only two of us in this town. *Sure,* I say, *soon as you tell me what it's for.*

Silence.

I gotta get out of sight. *That bad, huh?*

*Night,* he warns.

*Seems to me it's pretty relevant to what I'm doing,* I say, and activate my power with a sigh of relief.

My heritage gives me some interesting perks, and one of them is light manipulation. When I step out of the alleyway, almost no one can see me. I can still be tracked seismically or whatever, but light? Bends the way I want. I am in-fucking-visible.

Still gotta keep moving. Scott won't need sight to catch me if he gets in range. *It's the bank my client broke into, you know. So what is this thing?*

*Too big for you. Bring it back.*

Oh, fuck you. *She didn't seem to think it was,* I say, because now I'm feeling stubborn. *This the job you took earlier today, right after I took on Grey? That's some interesting timing.*

*Night, I mean it. You don't have a clue what you're dealing with.*

I pause, pressing against the wall so innocent folks don't walk into nothing and get spooked. *This* does *have something to do with why Grey was in that bank, doesn't it?*

*Night, I can't tell you that.*

*The cases are linked. What's going on, Scott?*

Silence.

*I need a reason,* I say, evenly.

Scott sighs. *This is pointless. Where are you? I'll come to you. We'll work together. Okay?*

*Tempting.* It is. I don't know what I'm into, and he does. *No can do right now, though. Talk later. I got tails.* Because I do. Three of the little blue dots have gone red. They followed me, taking the turns I did, and entering that alley.

Scott inhales. *Run. We'll talk when you're free.*

*Sure. Cassilda, keep an eye on them.*

*I've got your back,* says the most fantastic assistant in the world, and I take off at speed.

# CHAPTER 4

# CONSTRUCT

'm out of my mind, but hey—knowing your proclivities (and where you're likely to be dumb as mud) is practically a superpower.

*They've split,* said Cassilda, and I glance toward those red dots. They're still moving toward me (*far* faster than humans can move), but only one is on my trail directly. The other two are flanking, heading to parallel streets. They clearly got some kind of pincer move in mind.

When in doubt, stop going sideways. Down is the undercity, flooded with water and Dagon's people, so I ain't doing that. Up works. I mean, I can't fly or nothing, but neither can my tails, or they would'a come down on me from the sky. At least, I think so.

Easy to climb, all this old brick and old buildings, easy to find fingerholds humans never considered and pull myself up. Lizard-like, I scale the wall, and crouch on the roof. *Check.*

*Targets A and B came to a stop, as if losing track of you. Target C is still heading your way.*

I can see that, the red dot coming toward me. There's a good chance I'm still being observed by *something,* so I don't stick around to be caught. I take off.

Not my first time running across rooftops.

My magic keeps me hidden from most human technology, but Boston's got a healthy non-human population, so there's magical things up here, too —observation stones, wavering spells that reflect the passing-by of a living presence, and more. There's also laws about what kind of traps people can leave these days, so I don't expect much trouble as long as I don't linger.

C is still pacing me down below, though, and that's worrying. I take a minute to hold that package in my hand and magically suss it out.

It feels like nothing. It's just brown wrapping, faux-paper, kept closed with ordinary green twine. They went low-tech with it, and—

Wait. That's *real paper*. And the color isn't for the sake of old-timey aesthetics. It's *aged*. Maybe even slightly burned. What the actual hell am I holding?

*Target C is has climbed above street level and is three buildings behind you.*

Time to go faster. I can *move* when I need to, even in a fucking suit. Scott called me a young lion once, "loping along like some predator across the veldt." I decked him over it. Still pretty proud of that.

Maybe there's some clue what I'm supposed to do with this package written on the wrapping. Maybe—

*Target C is gaining.*

Damn. Okay, if I'm going all-out and they're still catching up, then they're *gonna* catch up, so it's time to switch strategy before I run out of juice.

Is the tail following me or the package? One way to find out. I duck behind one of those state-sponsored falcon perches—fortunately empty this time of year—and place the package down at one end while I squat low at the other.

And Target C lands on the roof.

That's a *big* thud, heavier than expected, and annoying because if they've been doing that the whole chase, there'll have been complaints, and that means law enforcement's gonna be part of this sooner rather than later. Fuckin' hell, that's clumsy.

They stop, and approach, and they... uh.

Um?

*Cassilda, what the fuck is that thing?*

*Unknown, boss.*

Yeah, I'll bet it is. This thing is deflecting light like I do, which means I can see it, but it is not using magic at all.

It's like some robot from one of those old movies. Smoothly walking on six legs, metal joints angled out from its body like a bug's. I can't tell where its sensors are, if it sees everywhere, if it's detecting air vibrations, or what. This is some kind of *construct*—and if I were not what I am, I couldn't see it at all.

This is human military shit, or I'm a pigeon. What in hell am I carrying?

I shift.

It turns slightly to face me.

It doesn't face the package, which means it's me the thing is tracking. Could be the vibrations from my heartbeat, the way my breathing disturbs the air, anything.

Gotta think fast. It hasn't attacked, so either it's not sure where I am with precision, or it's trying to lull me into making a mistake, or maybe it doesn't want to risk damaging the package by damaging me.

"Detective Night," it says in a voice I don't recognize. "You are in possession of an illegally acquired item, designated KR-45928. Turn over the item, and you will be released."

Sure I'd be released, having witnessed this definitely legal machinery running around and damaging rooftops.

Very carefully, I retrieve the package.

The construct turns toward me, not that it has a face, but there are tiny black holes I'm pretty sure shoot something nasty. "You got a warrant?" I say just to say something.

"Garner vs. Morimoto provides the precedent for one to retrieve one's purloined goods," it replies.

Which means *no*, but they've got a point. "Sure," I say, moving a little further from the empty falcon nest, and the construct turns toward me again. "There's a legal case to be made for violence in chasing down stolen things—except you got a problem, pal, 'cause I ain't stolen nothing, and I can prove that."

"You are guilty of collusion and theft," says the voice. "This is your last warning."

Collusion with who?

Ah; I get it. There is no way in hell they're gonna go after the Lins. So. I guess I'm today's patsy.

Question is *why*. Were they watching the bank, waiting for the courier? Were they just nearby enough to be informed of the package moving, and I got set up?

It hits me like cold water. I wasn't set up. *Scott* was set up.

That makes me fuckin' mad. "Interesting," I say, shifting carefully. "So how about we all go down to the police station together, nice and calm, and get this sorted out?"

Instead of answering, the thing shoots.

It's a fucking laser, light and heat, and Scott would be in real trouble handling it... *but I ain't Scott.* Light? Heat? My fucking ballpark, and I just absorb it.

Unfortunately, the thing knows at once that didn't work, and it lunges at me.

Lunges *fast*.

So much human tech is light and quick; most of it gets mounted on drones. The weight of this thing is *intentional*, and if this was a sting for

Scott, it makes sense. He's one tough mother; he wields shadows like hammers, and could fight this thing.

That's not the way I'm tough, so I run.

This thing pounds after me, clearly not giving a damn what damage it does. What the fuck is *in* this little folded bit of brown paper?

"Stop in the name of the Association!" it calls after me.

The what? *Cassilda! Can you hack it?*

*Analysis of its network is not yet complete.*

Shit. "Barnes vs. the United States gives me the right to defend myself with force in the face of ideological and manifested threat!" I shout as I run, which is the fancy way of saying we got ourselves a clash of Peoples and it's come to blows.

"We're aware," it says so fucking smugly, and tries to shoot me again, this time with some kind of projectile.

I ain't bullet-proof, but this one mostly misses because I just dive over the roof's edge. I can't risk getting cornered, so it's down to the ground, the stripe on my arm burning where it got me, and my heritage comes in real handy because what they shot was coated in some kind of poison.

Scott is tougher than I am, but he can't neutralize that. I can. This was definitely a sting for him.

On the flip side, I can't use shadow-stepping like he could, so now, it's a race. I'm just about out of options. They came prepared. The next thing they send after me will be set up for *my* weaknesses, so this is my shot to get away.

*Scott!* I communicate, because rivals or no, I definitely don't hate him. *It was a trap for you!*

*Get somewhere safe!*

*Naw, I was thinking of holding a bake sale,* I snap, and dodge another gunshot.

Glass breaks, and someone screams.

Okay. Whoever this Association is, they're willing to risk public property damage and possible innocent injury just to get what they think I'm carrying.

I barrel down the street as fast as I can. A vehicle crashes behind me. More shouts. Approaching sirens.

The law won't get here on time, and I got a bad feeling this Association isn't afraid of it, anyway. I don't wanna do this. Don't like this route, but I don't see another way right now. I'm gonna have to go underground. Whatever's in that package, I hope it can stand getting wet.

*The enemy is closing in. Forty feet.*

No time like the present. *The maintenance hole I'm looking at—*

*Unlocked and opening, boss.*

She's already hacked it. *Cassilda, I love you.* I leap without hesitation into the round, black hole in the street, leaving civilization behind, trusting her to close the cover behind me.

I land hard in the dark on an unseen surface in water up to my ankles. That's fine. I make my own light, and take off into complex tunnels dug by desperate rich people when they thought they found a way to cheat the consequences of the climate crisis they'd wrought.

These tunnels sure as hell ain't owned by them anymore.

The horrible screech of bent metal behind me says this Association is coming after me in the dark. Fine by me. It's time to see how helpful Ganymede can be.

Not even trying to be quiet, I run.

# CHAPTER 5

# UNDERCITY

It all changed for humans in the New Delhi Incident. Red and black dragon clans faced a prophesied new ruler, decided *nope,* and went to war.

I dunno what broke that night. What spells failed, or were never fired. Before anyone knew what was happening, dragons were revealed to the human Earth—which was supposed to be neutral and *ignorant* territory.

There was no hiding magic after that, and the other Peoples had to sort out when and how to reveal themselves. It got *real* messy, not just for the Ever-Dying who now had to deal with non-human persons and magic they could neither see nor control. It also got messy for the other Peoples, who'd been officially living on the three *other* worlds and not dicking around with this one.

*Unofficially,* they all had holiday homes here, investments and portfolios and small cities' worth of servants and slaves, and now everybody *knew* they did, and that all had to be worked out, too.

This is one of those places that got worked out.

The tunnels don't follow the rules up above. No human law judges this place. No humans even come down here, though they built it before the sea-rise took the undercity over.

Sea retreated as the Sun helped out. But by then, these tunnels had a new owner.

The clanging of that thing's feet are far too close. It *will* catch me if we just keep things going like this, but good news: things are about to go utter fucking sideways.

There is no warning before the unseen floor drops away.

I dunno how Dagon's people did it; this looked the same as every other part of these tunnels, three inches of water in bare, bleak hall. There was absolutely no way to know when it'd plunge me into cold, wet darkness.

Ah, but my ride's not over. *Finally,* I think as something grabs my ankle and yanks me down, deep, deeper down.

I'm dragged through water, through tunnels, through a blackness and chill so deep that even if I used my light, I wouldn't see anything but impenetrable ocean. I keep my eyes closed against the salt water, and I know it won't last long. I tell myself that, counting down in my head, holding my breath and not trying to fight.

The grip on my ankle tightens, and I'm whipped abruptly out of the water and thrown onto a rough rock berth. I tumble, losing a little skin, but I get up damn fast, because I know what's coming next.

Right behind me, that damned six-legged construct gets whipped out of the water, too, and thrown into the wall next to me. It smashes, pieces flying, and I shout, covering my face.

My rescuer stands in darkness across the water, which he controls like an extra limb. Several tube-like conjurings undulate between us, H2O made strong and solid, maintaining a nervous barrier. "You dare pursue a friend of the Sea?" howls a voice that isn't high or low or girl or boy or sound or sense.

Instead of answering, the damned robot tries to shoot me again. Either it's programmed in a loop, or whoever's controlling it is *real* determined I don't talk about what I saw today.

One of the water-arms whips overhead, grabs the construct, and squeezes. *Crunch.* Sparks. Pieces of unidentifiable metal ting away into the shallows.

The construct argues in a distorted and failing voice: "You are damaging Association property. According to the case of Zane vs. the State, you—" One last tortured wheeze, and the construct explodes.

And just like that, I got the time I need to make better plans than *go into the water-god's home.*

Before me, barely visible as an undulating wave in the darkness, is Ganymede Galene. Offspring of Dagon, high priest of the Boston Undersea, One With the Water, Master of the Damp Portal between this place and the multi-dimensional wonder of the oceans...

And utter nerd with too little self-confidence to believe any of the fifty-nine people who've tried to marry him actually gave a damn, and hired me to figure out who was "lying" and who was "the real one." You work that closely in a weirdo situation like that, you really get to know a guy.

"Shit," I say, shaking off pieces of shrapnel from my poor, ruined suit. "The fuck, Gany! Some of us have to buy clothes."

"Sorry!" he says back, and the water-arm sprinkles more metal shards along the stone and onto me. "Sorry, sorry! I thought you were in trouble."

"I was." And I still am. Like I said, you get to know a guy—and if I show any weakness here, in the heart of his little domain, he will eat me. It won't even be personal. I shake out my jacket, just scowling like I'm annoyed and not actually bleeding from a thousand cuts. "Thanks. I owe you."

"Sure," says Ganymede, whose body is made of water, whose essence is made of pure and constant willpower. "Owe me what?"

"Equivalent exchange, Gany, whatever that turns out to be," I say, tugging my sopping-wet lapels down and subtly making sure I still have the package. Damn, I hope it isn't destroyed. "Shit. I lost my hat."

The water bubbles, a rushing sound, and one of his water-limbs lifts my sodden mess of a hat from the water. My poor fedora. It's fucked. He holds it out, and though I can't see any expression over there, I'm pretty sure he's guilty. "Sorry about that," he says.

I snatch my hat. Best I can do is wring it out and stick it in my pocket; whatever structure it had is already wrecked. "Could be worse."

"What was that thing, anyway?" says Ganymede, gesturing toward the wreckage.

"Fuck if I know. You ever heard of the Association?" Careful not to give away that I've got multiple wounds to heal, I crouch over the shrapnel and pick through it, hoping to find something of use.

"Yes, actually," says Ganymede, who realized through my help that fifty-seven of those suitors actually cared about him when he'd fantasized there'd be only one (the *right* one), and proceeded to lock himself in a water tank to cry for a week. Yeah, that's right. People caring about him sent him into crisis. We can't all be made of arrogance and money like Nate Scott.

"Oh?" I take a moment to slag one or two suspiciously homogenous mechanical bits that could still be broadcasting.

"It's one of those all-human groups," says Gany, glorping closer to the edge of his stone shore. My light dances through him, casting happy prisms on the back wall. "Apparently it's been around for a few centuries? I don't know. I heard from the grapevine. By the way, Papa's here."

And *that's* why I didn't want to risk coming down here. "Is he?" I say, as mildly as I possibly can.

Gany splashes, a happy sound. "Yeah! You know he wants to see you again."

I'll bet he does. "Later. After this case."

"You have time to say *hi*," Gany insists.

"I don't," I say. "Visits with your Papa last a few days, bud. You know that."

He sighs heavily. No, I don't know how a giant sentient pool of water does that, either.

I pocket a couple pieces from this construct. "Any chance you can let me out at Harvard Square?"

"Papa's leaving tomorrow," Gany whines.

Which is real good, because the humans *do not know* there's a fuckin' god with a tendency to make half-him offspring running around Boston today. I can't imagine how wild that'd make the streets and cops and the rest up there. Besides, Gany has no sense of time, and if Dagon gets hold of me, the party will be on, and I really *will* be stuck for days in this fucking wet pit. "Gotta take a rain check, bud. This case has an expiration date."

"Okaaay," Ganymede says, all drooping water and sad, wet sounds. "Harvard Square?"

"Mass and Brattle, if possible," I confirm. "Then you got my word I'll come back and we'll hang out."

"With your spouse?" Gany says, hopeful.

Ha! He'd love *that.* "Sure thing. It'd be a gas." Sure it would! "I appreciate the help, twice over."

Gany borbles, pleased. "Anytime, my friend. Take a deep breath," he warns, and grabs around my waist.

And it's back in the water, pressing that inner pocket safe against my chest, eyes shut and breath held, and boy *howdy* do I feel it when we pass right by *Papa*, when Dagon the Golden Patriarch eyes me up, when I feel the thought-stuttering presence of a being called a *god* because what the fuck else could he be, and holding my breath is suddenly more nerves than necessity—

And miracle of miracles, he lets me go. I'm panting on the sidewalk as Gany retreats beneath the street hole cover, and woohoo, I made it.

Stiff, I stand and lean against the wall, and finally take a moment to heal my scrapes and bruises. I'm in Cambridge now, near the Charles River divide. There used to be tons of cutesy little shops here, and expensive homes, but seven feet of ocean-rise changed all that. Now, it's not a nice area, and humans don't really hang in this place unless they got *proclivities.*

Fine by me. I can hold my own well enough. More than that, though, I need to make damn sure this Association can't track me down before I get the chance to do something with... whatever this package is.

I can't go home; won't risk the spouse. Don't have any coworkers to go to. Law enforcement is right out—fuck knows what *they'd* do with this situation.

So: this part of Cambridge has got some contacts. Some folks who owe me favors. I'd say it's time to collect.

# CHAPTER 6

# A LITTLE OUTSOURCING

It ain't the first time I've walked into Jack's Place looking like something that got chewed up and spat out.

The few patrons in here pause and glance my way; some of their eyes gleam like a tiger's. Happily, it's obvious I'm not here to pick a fight, and they all go back to staring into their steins like they're searching for higher meaning.

Me, I walk slowly to the bar.

Jack waits for me there. He's a slim man, a black man about as wide as a broomstick, drying a clean glass because that's what bartenders do in old movies. His eyes don't gleam from *tapetum lucidum.* Nope—his irises glow green all on their own, which is a damned spooky sight in his unlit section of this bar. "I'd say look what the cat dragged in," he says in his surprisingly big and resonant bass, "but I think maybe 'look what the catfish drowned' might be more appropriate."

"Ha-ha," I say, dripping. "You got a minute?"

Jack eyes me.

We've had some fun as I tried to figure out how old he is and where he's from (I haven't), but I am too damn wet and too damn irritated to play that game right now, so I just stare back.

"There a reason you didn't just dry yourself off?" he says.

"Yeah. Heating up whatever's in the seawater under the city would make me smell like a dead whale," I say. I could've evaporated it, sure, but at what cost?

"Fair enough," says Jack, and puts down the glass he was pointlessly polishing. He nods at the door.

A little gust of wind closes it, flipping the sign out there from *open* to *closed*. None of the patrons even bother to look up.

"This way," says Jack in that *basso profundo* voice that has to have folks on their knees for him. "Elias! Take over for me." Elias—some grunt I don't know—gets up looking teenage-irritated and steps behind the bar. Jack, meanwhile, walks around the wall of pretty booze-full bottles, and disappears.

I follow.

Jack owns this whole corner. He's a Night-Child—a vampire, if you will —and nobody knows how long he's been around, but he's got a lot of clout among certain types of people. My types of people, specifically.

Takes no sides. Trades fair and easy. Keeps secrets. Got his fingers in more pies than there *are* people in this town, and he's always good for a deal.

You meet a person who doesn't screw you over, who keeps his word without the rigamarole of three-times an oath, and *that's* a professional relationship you want to keep.

We walk down a quiet, dull hall, one that obviously used to be for deliveries and other shit. The only light is what I bring myself; he doesn't need it. "Got quite a mood out there," I observe.

"Search group," he says.

"More missing Kin?" I frown.

"Yeah. Some fourteen-year-old kid this time. Never found her."

Shit.

This has been going on for three years now, and there's two minds on the missing kids: one, that's urban life, and people *go* missing. Two, the one I believe, is that though it hasn't been quick, and hasn't been many, it's Kin that's being targeted by someone who's careful not to trigger serial killer status.

I hate smart bad guys. Really, really do. "Cops still useless?"

"Cops think they all ran away. Tell me what you need."

In other words, stick to the plot. "Sure. New clothes, magical item analysis, and some answers if you got 'em."

"Analysis of?" he says, turning to the left to unlock a door with an honest-to-gods set of keys on a keyring.

"Something mechanical and something I'm unsure about," I say. "Discretion required."

He nods and enters the room.

It's your basic modern lab. Bright lights reveal numerous tables, loads of floating holographic whatsits, several active bubbling things and one spinning frog suspended in the air that looks like he's about to puke fire.

"Analysis has a high cost," Jack says.

"Yeah, I know," I say.

"You might be back to owing me. You sure you want to do that?"

Which means this one favor might eat up all the favors I've banked for the last year. Damn it.

I sigh. "Don't really got a choice."

"You know, that's a bad bargaining practice," he says, clearing space on a white table. "Telling someone they've got you over a barrel."

"Only if you trust the other guy not to fuck you dry."

He smiles and pats the table. "Show me what you've got."

Yeah, yeah. I place the package down. The paper is soaked and ruined; I feel a little bad about that, seeing as it was real, and old. Not my problem, though.

He eyes it. "Inert?"

"Dunno. It hasn't done anything so far. At least one baddie's come after me for it. Then there's these." And I drop the two handfuls of ruined metal beside the package.

"At least these are easy," says Jack, and taps the table by the first one. "I know that. It's Association tech."

Shit. "You've heard of them? Who are those guys?"

He crosses his arms and leans on the table. I like his brown suit; like me, he always opts for older styles, for casual colors and materials that speak to an older era in spite of the modernity of our surroundings. "We're getting into nasty territory here. Are you sure you're not being tracked?"

"I don't think so. They had me in sight, but since I lost them, they haven't caught up again." I indicate the machine pieces. "I couldn't sense anything happening here, or with this." And I indicate the package.

"Magical?"

"I don't know yet, but I assume so."

"Association and unknown chicanery," he murmurs as if toting up a list. "You can have the clothes and go, or you can go back into debt with me and get more."

We both know what I'll choose. "Rather learn who's trying to shoot me in the head, if it's all the same to you."

"Fair enough." He turns, waves his hand over a blank section of wall, and turns back around with a proper Fey black stone and an old-fashioned tablet. The stone, he sweeps over the metal and over the package. "You're right," he says. "Nobody's tracking either of these."

Relief is heavy within me. "That's a load off my mind."

"Now. The Association. I know them better than most because they don't like my family very much." And he taps the tablet.

An image appears in the air, projected between us: it looks like one of those old-fashioned wax seals in red. Before I struggle too hard to make it out, it lifts in three dimensions away from that seal so I can see the lines.

THE ASSOCIATION, it says in two concentric circles. CIRCA 1938. PRÓ IMPERIÓ HOMINUM AETERNÓ.

I haven't thought in Latin since the orphanage. Takes me a minute. "This is basically saying it's for the eternal empire of humans," I say.

"That's correct," he rumbles.

I'm gettin' a real bad feeling, like cold, fluxing water under my skin. "1938? That's hundreds of years ago."

"That's correct," he rumbles again.

I look at the ruined mechanical whatever on the table. "You recognized it right off."

"Because of this." He waves the black stone over the pieces again.

Both pieces disintegrate. Fall apart, into little piles of dust.

I stare at them. "Dead nanos?"

"Yep."

I literally only know what that looks like from history classes. "That shouldn't happen. They repair themselves."

"Not the Association's," says Jack. "Most nanos use Fey tech, which means magic is built-in—they repair no matter what happens. These don't have that benefit. They're pure human design, and have a built-in self-destruct if they can't repair themselves because their creators don't want the science stolen."

Magicless tech? Nobody would want it! More expensive *and* less versatile *and* fucking fragile? "The hell use would they even be?"

"Doesn't matter," says Jack. "The Association actually believe we want *their* technology, so they act with prejudice."

Lunacy. Human tech is *okay*, but really? It's Fey tech that matters, and it's everywhere. Of course it is; nobody makes it as good as they do, and for anyone to refuse it on grounds of... "Wait. They're refusing Fey tech just because it's got magic?"

"Because it isn't *human.*"

Which is a yes.

A whole lot of ugly pieces are coming together into an even uglier puzzle, and I wish I could send this one back for a refund. "So I take it they wanna wipe out everybody but themselves? Real doomsday cult?"

"Officially? Not at all. They research, finding ways to protect and help humanity. In reality? You should know their focus is Kin."

Of course it is. "Ruined human offspring?"

"Something to that effect."

No wonder they don't like Jack's family. Humans who *become something else* have gotta terrify these people, and that only happens with Night Children. "So. So, the search group out there…"

He sighs. "There is no evidence anyone can find linking the disappearances to the Association."

Which means people looked. "They're real careful about not leaving fingerprints, huh?" I say, my heat literally rising with my anger at some group taking out *children* for not being *pure enough.*

"Officially, they're neutral. Research. Unfortunately, they're also well-connected. They may operate under the radar, but poking that nest tends to bring bears out of the woods. Quite frankly, I don't want their attention. Even when they lose, they make a gods-damned legal mess," he says.

Which makes a few things real damn clear to me. One, they must be *real* under the radar, because I never heard of them before today, and that means the Association has not quite reached *word on the street* status. Two, the lack of caution from the construct that came after me shows desperation. They really want this package, even if it means blowing some of their cover.

Three, they really want Scott with it. He's no child, but he is Kin—Garnet-rated like me, no slouch. They'd planned to hit him hard and fast before he could shadow-step away. It would've been over, and nobody would even know why he didn't come home.

"You were right about the dead-whale stench," says Jack, because I'm steaming these clothes without meaning to. "Hang on a moment." He goes and rummages in a drawer.

I gotta calm down. Won't think clearly if I'm this fucking mad. "They want this thing, whatever it is. I need to open it up. I have no idea what's gonna pop out."

Jack turns around, folded clothes in hand. "Did you bring trouble to my door, detective?"

"Not on purpose, if I did," I say, since it's the truth.

He hands me the clothes and points. "Clean up. I'll set up a safe box."

The little washroom suits me just fine. As I bathe, getting all the under-city off me, I reach out to my spouse. *Hey.*

*Hey.*

That awkward pause of an intimacy strained by recent disagreement.

*You okay?* I say.

*It's been a challenging day. Work is terrible.*

*Bad client?*

*Competition is being a pain today, too.*

I dry myself instantly, steaming, and pull on the clothing Jack provided: shoes, socks, and boxers, simple slacks, and a button-down shirt. No jacket or tie. I feel naked. *Yeah? Something you wanna talk out?*

*Later. When you're home, and we can do it without the world between us.*

Always so dramatic. *Be careful. I love you, asshole.*

*I love you, too, my lion.*

If Scott weren't sincere, that wouldn't play, but he is, so. So I take a minute before heading back out, and make sure my eyes are real dry before I go.

Jack's set up a whole lot more than I expected.

The table is gone. In its place is a disc, some kind of gleaming white floor surface glinting with the barrier it's raised. The package hovers in the center of it, about a meter in the air. To the left is a projection—a three-dimensional bust of two people, peering down at it.

Jack is talking to the people in a language I don't know and have never heard before.

For one moment, the two turn and look at me, their eyes bright green and glowing, their ancestry *possibly* East Asian like mine—and though they aren't really here, I absolutely feel the weight of their matching gaze.

"Thanks," says Jack.

"We await results," says the smaller of the two.

"With eagerness," says the taller, and the projection disappears.

Wow, who the heck were those? "Outside consult?" I say, trying to keep it mild.

Jack nods, explains nothing, and studies the little package. It sits there, wrapped in wrecked brown paper, inert. "They believe it will be safe to inspect," he says.

"They better be right, then," I say.

"They may be," he says with complete calm. "Let's start with gauging its power level, if there is one." He takes up a black Fey stone and waves it over the package... and the stone cracks.

Jack startles and drops the pieces, which bounce off the floor in opposite directions.

"The fuck!" I say, stepping back.

"So," says Jack, his low voice smooth, "it's very powerful."

"Oh, good," I say.

"It overwhelmed the detector, is what it did," says he.

"Oh, good," I say.

"Night." He looks at me. "These stones are rated to Celestial. Do you understand what that means?"

I do. It means whatever this thing is, it's bigger than Celestial-rated beings, which includes people like the Raven King. And if it's bigger than the Raven King... "It belongs to a god."

"Or was made by one, or a whole host of other possibilities," he says.

"Oh, good," I say a third time, and now I'm even more concerned why a group so dead set against the esoteric would want this thing.

If they'd wanted it destroyed, they'd have tried a lot harder to destroy me. Fuck. I need to know. I need to know what in hell it is.

Jack waits, looking at me.

"Safe to unwrap it?" I say weakly.

"For me and the world? Yeah. For you? I don't know."

Right. I take a deep breath and step into the white circle.

All the sound cuts off. It's a proper barrier.

A pinch of my magic snaps the twine. Carefully, leaning back, I unfold the paper like a weird flower.

Lying in the center is a single broken piece of mirror.

Its edges jagged and black with age, it reflects the ceiling, innocent and clear. It is absolutely *not* innocent, and I have no idea what'll happen if I look into it.

Jack steps into the barrier and peers at it, arms crossed. "Ominous," he says.

"No kidding. Any ideas?"

"Not my department."

"Yeah," I say, staring at it. "That's fair. Thank you. I'm sorry if I did end up bringing trouble to your door."

"Don't fret," he says in that bass I can feel in my toes. "If there is trouble, it'll follow you out."

True enough.

All of this fuss over a broken piece of mirror. Wild human-centered groups. The Lin family. A scheme involving Scott, somehow? Why Scott? Because he's Kin? So am I. So's a lot of Boston. What's the big deal? And how, for the love of hell, does all of this go back to Grey and the Raven King?

What do I do with this thing? "Thanks, Jack."

"Thank me after you've paid me," he says, and steps away.

"Got anything I can use to wrap this mirror up again?"

"Sure." He tosses me a little sack, soft and thin and magically reinforced. "That should keep it from breaking further."

If paper could hold it, this surely can. I use the bag like a glove and pick the piece up, securing it. It goes into my back pocket. "I better get going."

"Good luck, Night. Be careful. People high in the human government belong to the Association, and have for centuries. If you fall afoul, getting out of that won't be easy."

*If* I fall afoul. Too late for that. "Thanks. Let me know when you need a favor back."

"Believe me, I will," says Jack, his bass mellifluous, his expression neutral.

Cassilda and I check five times to ensure I'm not being followed before I leave through Jack's back door.

# CHAPTER 7

## GETTING A HEAD

got two ways to go here. One, in ignorance, on the run, seeing if I can find someone powerful enough to handle this mirror-situation and maybe provide some protection. Two, risk it all to grab Grey by his leaf-thin ears and shake the truth out of him.

All right, all right, *some* of this is on my head. I didn't have to go along with Lin's case of mistaken identity... except I actually *did*, because if I'd walked away from it, Scott would be dead, and I wouldn't even know what the hell happened.

I didn't have to hang on to this mirror after, either... except I actually *did*, because who knows what a group like The Association might do with a magical item so dangerous they're willing to risk centuries of regulation to obtain it?

My gut instinct is good, but it don't care too much for self-preservation.

I could give the mirror up now. Go get Scott, get out of Dodge. Between us, we've got enough money to start elsewhere, if we wanted. Except we can't do that. We'd be followed; I know that for damn sure. We'd never be able to settle down. Besides, I gotta know what's happening, gotta know why, gotta know what's coming.

Scott understands that. Heck, he's said that's one of the reasons he fell for me.

Fuck. I miss him. Gotta snap out of it. Thinking about him right now is gonna make me slow. *Cassilda. Load message number four-five-eight. You know what to do.*

*Got it, boss.*

If I die, she'll send it off to my husband. I just... I want him to know I love him, you know?

Anyway. Moping done. It's time to decide what I'm gonna do next.

So that's how I end up at the jail dressed like a dame.

If I go as myself, and if the Association is as deep in this as I fear, some A.I. somewhere might flag me. This idea, though? This one always works.

Law enforcement rarely admits non-humans in this town, and the kind of folks who seek this job tend to also be the kind who insist on imaginary "traditional" gender roles. When I'm dressed as a dame, I don't get the same kind of suspicion I would if I went in as me. I'm automatically weaker, see?

Helps that I'm hot, of course.

I'm Chinese by blood, but if I'm gonna play into people's biases, I'm going all the fuck out: bleach-blonde, red lipstick, tight little red dress, leaving *no* doubt whatsoever that I got parts these guards would be interested in, and because they want my smile and my favor, because a sweet little smirk is more effective than cash in hand, they're gonna let me in.

All I gotta do is ask right, and smile, and bat my eyelashes, and hint at things by thrusting out my illusionary chest. "Please let me see him," I say, my eyes all big and liquid. "I know it's not visiting hours, but... please."

"Really shouldn't," says guy one to my nipples.

"Please? Can someone give me permission, maybe?" I say, pouting my tempting red lips.

That guy gets someone else, who spends a little while telling my breasts it just isn't done that way, and then *that* guy gets someone else who apparently has authority. "Well," says guy three, looking me up and down, lingering, and checking my face to see if I mind (which I pretend I do not, and he's *happy* about that). "I guess it wouldn't hurt to give you half an hour. That good for you?"

"It's enough to tell him a piece of my mind. I never should've dated someone... like that," I say with sweet venom, and he laughs.

"Fey?" says guy three.

I nod. "I left my wheelhouse, and look where it got me?" I sniffle. "I'm so ashamed."

"Aw, we all make mistakes. Better learned sooner than later," says racist asshole three with something like tenderness, and leads me down the hall.

I have absolutely no doubt that if we weren't being observed, he'd cop a feel. Jackass.

"Half an hour," he says again, and opens the interrogation room.

I give him the sweetest smile, mouth *thank you*, then fake an angry little moue and step inside.

Whatever Grey was expecting, it was *not* me. "What?" he says.

"Hi, lover," I say as the door closes.

Spell time. I set this up beforehand; whatever they're listening to won't be what's actually said.

Grey sees through this guise, of course (which these idiots would have if they'd hired anyone magical), and looks shocked for all of one second. "Um."

I sit across from Grey. "We need to talk."

He leans in, looking fully chagrined, ears down. "About?"

"Figured it might do you good to *reflect* on your situation," I say, making direct and accusatory eye-contact.

He's pretty good. No physical tells but one: he goes pale.

So he knew it was a mirror. "Don't suppose you have any advice, *lover*," I say. "Maybe even some damn answers."

He swallows. "I take it you've ensured they can't hear us."

"Can't you tell?" I bat my eyelashes at him. "They're hearing a whispered lover's quarrel."

Grey exhales slowly. "How did you know about the mirror?"

"Hands-on experience."

He sputters. "What? How in hell did you see it?"

"It was literally handed to me. What is it, and what do I need to know?"

His jaw falls open. "*Handed* to you? They..." His eyes go so wide that I can see the entire dark limbal ring around his irises. "The Lins just *gave* it to someone?"

"Apparently so." We have so little time. I need to push him. "You don't have more get-out-of-jail-free cards this time, Grey. Answer my questions."

"Or what?" he blurts.

"Or I'm gonna turn you over to the Throne myself," I say calmly. "Drag you there by the balls."

He scrunches. There's no other word for it: scrunches, ears down, nose wrinkled, hunched in his seat. "That's a little nonconsensual, yeah?"

"So is sending a guy into a bonkers scenario with no information, the Raven King looming overhead, a humans-only group throwing tacks under the wheels, and a magical gewgaw of dubious province," I say.

His mouth works for a moment. "Humans-only? What? It all sounds so bad when you put it that way," he says in a tiny voice. "I just figured you'd stir up some trouble and draw attention away from me."

"They set up a sting for my rival, Scott," I tell him. "And Lin said something about a debt when she handed it to me."

He runs his hand through his long hair, looking so confused. "Who's they?"

"A group called the Association."

His brow knits. "Why is that familiar?"

"You tell me. What's going on, Grey?"

"I... I can't," he says.

"You can. There is gonna be a way you can, or someone you can direct me to with answers."

And the asshole says, "Well, there's Bran himself. The Raven King."

"Very funny."

"He'd answer you," he says.

"And probably rip out my spine to power his eternal youth machine," I point out.

"Hey!" Grey sits up, frowning. "That was his grandfather, not him. He doesn't use that."

"Sure he doesn't."

Grey sighs. "It only works with family, anyway, and—"

"Answers, Grey. Now." Of course I want to know more gruesome Darkness royalty secrets, but *priorities*.

He puffs, cheeks out, and leans back, and I see the exact moment he realizes he has to spill. "Here's what I *can* tell you: it's called the Mirror of Remorse."

"Friendly title." I lean back, too, arching a little to ensure whoever's watching this gets a shot right down my fake cleavage. "And it does what?"

"It shows you what you are, genetically." He leans forward, too, supposedly getting an eyeful of my imaginary mammaries. "For someone like me, I already know, so who cares? But you... you're Kin. Unknown, from some magical something or other, and unclaimed. When you look in that mirror, it shows you your non-human family. And if they're alive, they see you, too... and they'll know, within reasonable distance, where you are."

My turn to go pale. "They... they what?"

"Believe me, I *know* what a problem that is," he snaps, looking ashamed. "We don't have a good track record when it comes to viable offspring."

No. They don't.

Magical Peoples reproduce really, really slowly. Humans can make thousands more of themselves in the time it takes, say, a member of the Sun to create one—except when it comes to Kin.

We reproduce as fast as humans do. There've been times—largely before we became a People—that we got taken to 'shore up numbers,' whether or not we were willing.

*Boss,* says Cassilda. *Visual surveillance just cut out.*

*What? Any signs of trouble?*

*Not yet, boss. No alarms have been raised, and all the guards' vital signs seem to be calm.*

*Keep an eye on it.*

It can't be the Association. I'm being paranoid. How would they even know I was here?

Unless they were monitoring Grey in case I did exactly what I'm doing now. Shit.

Need to hurry. "This mirror pretty much guarantees a bad situation," I say.

He nods. "Yeah." He looks a little sick.

I *feel* a little sick. "Why are you dicking around with this? Why did they have it?"

He glares. "I'm not *dicking around* with anything. It's been carefully guarded for thousands of years, so you know."

"Great! And then they just handed it off to some guy?"

"I have no idea why they'd do that! They wouldn't give it to Bran no matter what he offered!"

Oh, what the hell is *that* about?

On the other side of the wall comes a *thump.*

We both look at it. The thump isn't repeated.

*Cassilda?*

*I can't see what it is, boss, but no alarms have been triggered.*

Oh, this whole thing is going south so damn fast. "Lemme guess. The Raven King wants it because he needs offspring, so he's looking for viable Kin."

"No, no, no!" Grey says, looking utterly offended as he sits up. "Bran wouldn't! He—" and he stops. Tries. Physically cannot continue.

So we've run right up against his oaths. All right, new direction. "Which has what to do with you showing up at the bank?"

"Oh. I was going to do that, anyway. Everything I told you about the marriage to—" The name fuzzes out, like my ears are too human to hear it —"is real. I had to get out of it, and me being arrested like this might just have done it. Her mother is *pissed*."

I stare. "And how was this mirror connected?"

He can't answer. He tries. Sighs. "Sorry. It's Bran's story to tell."

"Well, fuck him. I'm smashing it the second I leave this place."

"Oh, ah." He scrunches again. "That won't work. It can't be destroyed."

I frown. "It's already a fragment. Something destroyed it pretty good already."

"No, that's the shape it's meant to be," he says. "Part of the magic—representing that it's showing *part* of a whole person."

Fucking magical logic. If he says it can't be destroyed, he's probably right —and it explains why the Kin haven't. "I'm not turning it over to him."

"You should. He's the safest choice."

And Grey just confirmed Bran wants this, which means I can't let that happen. "I don't believe you."

Grey's voice drops. "He'd never lose it, and it would be perfectly safe with him."

A Fey prince, defending the Lord of Umbra? That makes no sense. People of the Darkness *eat* People of the Fey. "We're missing something. It makes no sense that—"

*The supervisor who led you in here is at the door, boss.*

I go real still. Someone knocks.

It hasn't been half an hour. "Why's he not just coming in?"

Grey frowns. "I don't know." His ears flick down.

A second knock.

Shit, shit, shit.

A third knock.

So I can think of one possible reason for this: they want one of us, or both, to *come to the door.*

Yeah, this has fallen apart. "I think we're in trouble," I warn Grey, standing.

He looks pale as he stands, too, tossing the handcuffs to the table. "Not exactly standard procedure."

"No shit."

The door opens.

There stands the supervisor. His face is blank, and his eyes are sort of *sunken.* He opens his mouth. "You are in possession of an illegally acquired item, designated KR-45928. Turn over the item, and you will be released."

You have got to be joking. "The fuck?" I say, my illusioned voice high and panicked.

"Nope," says Grey, and sings a note.

It's power. Such power, such raw, glorious power like I could never wield, Celestial rank or I'm a pumpkin, and it smacks the guy like a battering ram and sends him back into the hall.

"Shit!" I cry, stumbling backwards, my guise falling away.

"He was already dead!" Grey cries, his hair shifting to bright and lambent silver, his eyes gleaming and glowing as he prepares for battle. "We are in trouble!"

We sure are. Dealing with local government jent after this is gonna be a nightmare. "We gotta get out of here! And where are the damn alarms?" I snap. There are no alarms. They should be going off all over. What the hell happened?

*Boss,* says Cassilda. *The internal network has been shut down completely.*

That's a *great* sign.

There's a window. I could burn our way out. A fireball would be a fucking mess, but magical fire should —

"Oh my gods," moans Grey, and I have to see, to turn back around and see why.

So. The guard is dead, of course. But, uh. Grey didn't *detach his head.*

Nope. That noggin got free on its own, producing six metal legs exactly like that construct that attacked me earlier, and oh, boy, here it comes, mouth slack and flopping, eyes completely sunken in.

I admit it: I freeze. I agree with Odysseus—*everybody* deserves respect in death, even enemies—and this horror-show flips some switch in my brain so I just stare like a fool, like maybe it'll vanish if I look hard enough.

Then Grey sings some kind of battle-note and smacks it with sound. The centi-head goes tumbling backwards, leaving brain and blood and saliva in its wake, but it's a tough little bugger. It rights itself, sort of shakes like wet dog as it recalibrates, then comes at us again.

Nobody's coming to see what in hell is going on. There's no question the enemy has the compound. "Outside wall!" I say, pointing.

"Got it!" says Grey, and *sings.*

The wall explodes outward like it's made of glass.

I don't wait. I grab his arm and run.

Sonic weaponry goes off behind us, wielded by who knows what, but Grey's shielding works for both of us and it's shunted aside.

(It would drop human prisoners with pee in their pants and possible brain damage. None of it stops us. Every once in a while, I get why groups like the Association exist. They're scared. I understand *scared.* Though why they'd assume we're suddenly *more* of a danger to humanity than before and need to be taken out *now*—)

*Four drones, seventy feet above,* says Cassilda. *Internally networked. I need more time to hack them.*

"Drones," I warn Grey.

"Drones?" blurts Grey, shocked.

They're coming. But why are they so close? They should be trying to shoot us from a mile in the air.

Grey tries to sing, and can't because he's running. Ha! Someone's out of shape.

"What the fuck was that guy's head?" I pant, doing what I can to hide us both, at least from anything that requires light to see us. "What *was* that?"

"A nightmare!" he cries, and I can't argue. His ears twitch, and he suddenly dodges.

A little drone, not even the size of my palm, slams past his head at such speed it crashes into the ground, and we both see the six-inch needle sticking out the front of the thing like some horrible demon-dick, and I guess we got part of an answer as to what the fuck happened to that supervisor.

(So many questions. Does the Association have actual power over the jail? Was this illegal or supported by human government? Are they *this* desperate to get the mirror? Are they risking everything, or do they have the official nod?)

"We need to get out of here," Grey says, his eyes enormous.

"Yeah, we do," I say, but there are no street holes here, and we're too far to get into the river, and any building we go into, they'll just follow, and—

"Do *not* tell anyone about this!" Grey snaps, and produces something I don't understand. A coin? A round metal coin, stamped with the Throne and its weird-ass tendrils? And then—

So fast. Happens so fast.

He throws it down, *boom*.

White bars shoot out of it like beams of solid light.

He grabs my arm (and is strong enough to stop my forward motion, and I'm no lightweight) and pulls me in.

# CHAPTER 8

## FORTY-SIX SECONDS

We're falling. Sliding? Flying? Barrel-rolling?

This has to be a Fey portal. I've never taken one before, and it turns out all the horror stories are true.

There is *hungry emptiness* around us, an absolutely conscious void that would erase us for **being**, if it could, and we're rocketing down some frictionless path that feels like a greased blade. I can't even scream because I can't get air, and before I even have the chance to process what the *hell this is*, we're out.

Tumbling, onto the ground, or at least I am, in the least graceful landing I've had since I was a fucking toddler. I end up on my ass.

Grey stands over me, not a hair out of place, and tucks his coin away. "Shit."

Trees tower all around us. A pleasant breeze carries familiar scents of topsoil, leaves and loam. "Why in hell... Where the hell..."

*Boss, you're alive,* observes Cassilda.

*Yeah?* I say, and then I realize: she probably lost connection with me when we went into the portal. Which means... *You didn't send my farewell message, did you?*

*I did, boss. It was received and opened forty-six seconds ago.*

I groan. Shit. He's gonna think I'm dead. And I don't got time for spousal support right now because of this mess. *Cassilda, call—*

"This is really not ideal," says Grey, and crouches next to me. "I'm beginning to think we were both betrayed here, but that doesn't make any sense."

"Yeah, who'd do that to swell guys like us," I state.

"No need for snark," he says, stands, and offers his hand. "Sorry, for what it's worth. I really hadn't planned any of this to go south, and certainly not for you to get hurt."

That's a clear admission of fault. Fey culturally don't do that. This guy has really done some work on himself.

I'm shaky, so I take his hand. Dignity's got nothing on getting back my own two feet. "The apology's accepted, and appreciated, but it doesn't fix anything, you get it? We need to figure this out now."

*Spouse requests contact*, Cassilda says.

Yeah, I'll bet he does. "Gimme a second. Scared the shit out of my husband," I tell the Fey.

"Husband!" says Grey like he's just tuned in to his favorite show. "A hardcore fellow like you, tying the knot?"

I roll my eyes at him, then turn away. *Put him through.*

*—answer me, or I swear to gods—*

*Hey, you big galoob*, I send him, because I already know how this is gonna go, and all I can do is try to lighten it.

A pause. *You're... you're alive?*

He's choked up. Makes it harder to keep my cheery shtick going, but I gotta. *Yeah. Sorry about that. Got yanked into a portal, and Cassilda thought I was dead.*

*I thought you were dead! What portal? Where the hell are you?*

"I read up on you!" Grey says. "Nobody said you were married."

"Yeah, well, it's not public knowledge," I snap. *I'm not dead. Sorry to scare you.*

*I asked you where you are, Night.*

*And I ain't telling you, lover. This one's too dangerous.*

*Boss, spouse is attempting triangulation.*

Yeah, thought he would. *Block him.*

*Already on it, boss.*

Grey's grinning like a natural-born fool. "What's he like?"

"A brat," I say, and even in the middle of B.F.E., I can't keep the raw affectio n from my voice. *I can't let you come. I'll make it through this, lover. You wouldn't.*

*Don't you do this!*

*Already done. See you tonight.*

*Simon!*

*Cassilda, silence him. Record anything he says, though.* Because apparently, I want to suffer.

*On it, boss.*

Big stupid lump in my throat. Big stupid lug in my bed. He used my first name. He doesn't even do that when we're making love.

All right, Night, focus up. Feel bad about it all later.

Grey sighs, looking wistful. "Those are the best kind of spouses."

Wonder who he's thinking of? Clearly not the fiancé he's dodging. "Only if you're into dramatic demands. Where the hell are we?"

Grey winces prettily. "Just north. Not far. I think... Vermont?"

I stare. "Vermont."

"Yeaaaah?" he says and smiles, ears back and down.

For the love of hell. "Grey," I say carefully. "I need you to give me a reason—right now, and real good—not to go to do something absolutely in- sane, like shipping this stupid fucking mirror *into space*, because I swear to you that's about to happen."

He stares. "How would you even do that?"

"Grit." I bare my teeth.

He's all limpid eyes and droopy ears. "Maybe we should ask for help?"

"Ask who? The Raven King?"

"Bran's not so bad," he says.

"When, in bed?" I snap. "This is serious."

"So am I!"

I rub my face. "His kind eat your kind."

"Normally, yes," he says, sort of twisting back and forth like he's uncomfortable. "He's different, though."

Sure he is. "Why?"

"Well... Notte... might be involved?" says Grey, his eyes wide and innocent.

Notte. The Father of Blood. The original vampire, thousands of years old, Lord of the Night Whispers, and *absolute fucking recluse.* "Sure," I say. "I didn't clock you for crazy, but I guess here we are."

"Don't be rude," he says, crossing his arms.

"That ain't rude. You ain't *seen* rude. Hear what I'm saying now: we need a damn plan. What to do with this thing. How to get ourselves out of trouble—because believe me, they ain't gonna blame some weird, rich human group for what happened back there. It's coming down on my ass, and maybe yours."

"You aren't particularly known for removing and mechanizing people's heads," Grey points out.

"And that'll matter how much to some judge? A *plan*. And the only way to make that is if you fucking tell me what you can. All of it."

My anger falls pretty flat in this place. It's lovely; quiet winter trees, cries from the birds that don't migrate, a few small and inoffensive rustles in the bush.

Grey's look is unimpressed. He sighs—as though I'm the one who started all this—and he counts on his fingers. "The Mirror of Remorse. No one's really sure who made the thing, though they think gods might be involved because it can't be destroyed."

Confirmation. "How about conveniently lost?"

"They tried. It always comes back." He counts on his second finger. "It has one purpose: to quickly and easily identify any Kin."

"Yeah. I'm beginning to see why a group all about humans-only might want it, and I don't think it involves invitations from their stationery drawer."

He pales.

I hold up my finger. "Did Bran know it was in that bank?"

Loophole found: I guessed. He didn't *tell*. Relief blooms through him, releasing tension. "Yes."

"And he sent you in there to... scout the place?" Nothing. "Ensure it was there?" Nothing. "Test their security?"

He leans forward, but can't say.

Close. "To... bypass security? To..."

"The Lins are a very proud family," he says, sweating as if even that cost him.

Pride. Security. Leading to them choosing to offload the Mirror right away. "To demonstrate their security is shit? Maybe to prove they should give it to Bran?"

Relief. "You're good at this, detective."

"And you were already in town, going to do something insane *anyway,* so it was a favor."

"Yes!" he says, and droops. And I mean *droops,* hair limp, ears down, lower lip trembling. "I was already here, and running ideas by Bran for just what to do that might lock me up without making things too dire, and he suggested I help in this way."

"Uh-huh. So how did anybody else know where it was?"

He blinks. "I don't know. I can ask him."

What a clusterfuck. "So we have him mysteriously knowing where it is... and mysteriously, a Kin detective is hired to go pick it up for who knows what, which turns out to be a mysterious trap set up specifically to take him out *while* carrying that mirror."

Grey eyes me. "You really are smart, aren't you?"

"Naw," I say, 'cause I'm not feeling too clever right now. "Or I would not be stranded in B.F.E., talking to a runaway Fey prince about a cursed, indestructible mirror, with everyone in the worlds on both our tails."

"B.F.E.?"

"Butt-Fuck, Egypt," I explain.

He laughs wryly, then shakes his head. "I can ask Bran how he knew where it was. That might be relevant."

I exhale. "I don't like the idea of him knowing where *we* are. You really sure you can trust him?"

"Yes, of course."

"Why?"

He smiles crookedly. "I've known him for a very, very long time. He hasn't eaten me yet, even when I annoyed him."

"Probably to avoid war with your Throne," I point out.

He shakes his head. "No. It's because he's trying to be a good person, which is complicated. I really don't care if you don't believe me; it took him about a hundred years to actually convince me of this, and he's stayed true to it."

"Right." I rub my face. "The ruler of the Darkness. A good person."

"I mean, all things considered," he concedes.

"So you'd be willing to swear to me—with your honor and your credibility on the line—that you don't think he's being nefarious in all this."

"He wouldn't dare," says Grey. "Mr. Night, I'm positively offended on his behalf."

Part of being a good investigator is challenging your own bias. Hell, that's part of being an intelligent person. I don't know Bran. Grey does; Grey swears Bran's not like his grandfather was. I don't think Grey is lying. He may not be, but biases or not, it feels like too big a risk right now. "Just call me Night. We busted out of a prison together. Pretty sure that puts us on a less formal basis."

He tilts his head. "Not Simon?"

"Nobody uses Simon but my spouse."

That's a boundary, and he doesn't seem inclined to cross it. "Fair enough, Night. So. What do you want to do instead of asking for help from our best resource?"

I ignore the sarcasm. "The way I see it, the biggest issue is there's either a spy with the Raven King, or a spy with the Lins," I say. "More likely the Lins, but there's really no way to know yet. Someone told the Association too much, and the Lins must have owed a real unpleasant favor."

Grey looks a little stunned. "We might be out of our league, here."

"Welcome to my life." I pace. What to do, what to do?

Step one: I need to do something safe with this mirror. If I'm caught—which seems more likely than not right now—the wrong people will get it.

Step two: I need to clear my fucking name, but how? I have Cassilda's recordings, but they'll have their own, and it can take weeks to figure which one's been adjusted.

Step three: I need to keep Scott the fuck out of this. This was so... *perfectly* set up for him.

I stop pacing. That, in fact, bugs me a lot more than anything else here. Why him? It could've been a toss of the dice, sure, but why him? They could've picked anybody. The Lins have major contacts. Why in fuck did they choose Scott?

My gut instinct is almost never wrong. Maybe I'm just overtired, and feeling targeted, but I don't think so. I'm getting the weirdest feeling that maybe, somehow, this whole thing isn't about the mirror after all. It's about Nate Scott.

"Shit." I resume pacing again.

"Your face is a *story*," says Grey, watching me with fascination.

"Yeah, yeah."

"Seriously, I have *got* to know what you're thinking," he says, having, in my distraction, conjured a chair and table so he could prop his chin in his hands and watch me.

I stare. "The hell did you get those?"

He grins naughtily. "It's a trick. Automatic table and chair. Fun at parties."

Freaking Fey. "Sure. Okay. Okay, I have an idea... and it's a really, *really* shitty one." Because it is.

"What a salesperson," he says dryly.

I glare at him. "Yeah, well. Here's the thing. We both got ties to the city, and reasons we need to be there. Right? You with your whole... jail debacle, and me with my whole damn life."

"Sure," he says, eyeing me.

"Going on the run won't work." Though I want to. I want to just go grab Scott and fucking *flee*, but we can't. It would never last over time. The Ever-Dying are too good at surveillance, and I don't think either of us want to try to make a new life as Kin in one of the other worlds. "Not only that, but the longer they have to figure out what happened—what went wrong with their stupid plan—the longer they'll have to come up with a better one, and I don't got time for that. What I *do* got is people who owe me favors, a personal reason to get this solved, and a long fucking wick that they damn well lit."

"All right," he says slowly, and his long, fine ears are trembling. "You're sounding like, ah—no offense? But some sort of absurd hero about to charge the enemy fortress in a movie."

"Yeah, well. That's 'cause I am," I say, and take the mirror out.

His wide eyes go wider, and his whole body perks up. "You really want to show up at the gate without an army?"

"Yeah. You in?"

"No." There was no hesitation. "If I showed up, they'd assume violence, scuppering whatever your plan might be." He gets a keen look, a sharp look, a look worthy of a working mind. "Why would they talk to you instead of just killing you and looting your body?"

"Because they're gonna think I know where this is." I hold up the little bag with that mirror shard. "I'm setting a damn trap."

Grey looks pained. "I'm rather *for* trickery, you know, in general, but I don't think stubbornness is going to get you through this."

I ignore that. "I got a plan. Your part's real easy: tell Bran the mirror is going into retirement. No one's ever gonna find it. He can just relax."

He swallows. "That's a big assumption."

Yeah. "I know."

He exhales. "All right. If you're sure. But before you go... can I see it? Just once?"

I eyeball him.

"I swear, just to look. I'll swear it three times if you need."

"All right, all right." I hand it over.

He immediately dumps the bag into his hand.

"Oi!" I say.

"Wow," he says, and his hair rises, and his eyes glow like the moon, and light from fucking nowhere dances all over his face like some sunlit pond giving back. "Wow. It's... it's accurate." He slips the mirror back inside.

"Are you crying?" I say, staring at him.

Grey wipes his eyes; his pale skin has gone blotchy, a weirdly mortal and relatable thing. "I haven't seen my father in a very long time," he admits, and hands it back. "Long before he died."

Shit. "Regrets?"

"Oh... so many," he whispers.

I believe that, but it's a rabbit hole to leave behind for now. "Right. You head on to Bran, but before you do, can you drop me back in Boston?"

"Are you sure you want to do this? You might die," he says, tiny. "I don't want that."

"I don't want that either, but I've got to. There's no time for another way."

His ears don't droop; they're back, mid-point, taking me seriously. "All right. Where to?"

I tell him where I need to go. I even tell him why.
"Eugh. Good luck with *that*," he says by way of farewell.
Guess I can't blame him. Nobody *likes* the smell of fish.

# CHAPTER 9

# SALT

Any investigator worth their salt is gonna study the opposition, and lemme tell you, the Association's a slippery one.

I get Jack's frustration. They never break the rules in an obvious way. While their official ethos is absolutely dangerous—exclusionary and panicky, the kind of thing that leads to cults and coups—so far, in hundreds of years, all it's led to is a lot of scientific research into things like the human genome.

Which doesn't exactly line up with taking over prisons and sending six-legged robots to smash through streets, does it? So I dig further, and guess what I find?

Our little local branch of the Association doesn't get funding from the main hub anymore.

There is no record of what happened or why. They're just privately and anonymously funded now, as of about six years prior. It's still got the branding, too—but the address is no longer listed in the main Association hub. If I were a betting man, I'd say this had all the earmarks of a plausible deniability setup.

*Oh no, they went rogue*, would seriously not fly without the resources and legal weight the rest of the organization brings to the table, but here we are. If everything goes right for me, and this branch goes down, it won't so much as smudge the Association's nose.

It's still gotta go down. And just maybe they won't try this shit again if it goes down *real* publicly.

So. Plan formed. They get to break the rules? Then *so do I.*

I'm back under the streets of Boston, and it ain't even been six hours.

This time, there's no running. I take it slow, walking along the edge, making my own light. I whistle "My Bonnie Lies Over the Ocean," enjoying the sharp and distorting echoes, wishing my pants weren't fuckin' soaked to the waist in someone's idea of a joke.

The saltwater's relatively clean (has to be, since most of Dagon's kids breathe the stuff), but it's fuckin' *cold*, and there are these *deep* spots for no damn reason, so one second you're walking, and the next, you're up to your nips in ice.

The things I do for this job.

Plan A is to find Gany again. He's got a starring role; it'll help him out, and help me out, and ensure I'm not actually charging the gates without an army. Plan B is one I'm *not considering*, because the price would be a lot higher, but I'm not dumb enough to assume it couldn't happen.

So I walk, and I call. I walk, and I wait. I make my own light (like I do) and whistle. And—

**You seem lost, little fella,** teases the voice I was *not considering*, the voice that comes from every direction, that swallows my thoughts and buzzes my blood, that vibrates with good, deep humor that almost makes his overbearing, overwhelming, orgy-having self bearable.

Gany never showed. Papa did. Lucky me. Plan B, it is. "Hello, sir. Good to see you again."

***Thought for sure you wouldn't come back 'til I left, what with you told my kid,*** he says, all casual, his oddly deep-country drawl heavy.

"Well, I'm still on that case, sir," I say, not really looking anywhere in particular because he *is* the "where" right now, both the water and the tunnels holding it like immortal veins. "I'm heading into the showdown now, and wouldn't you know it? I came up with a plan, a scheme, a real *memorable* time, if you will, that you might like, so I thought I'd invite you along."

***Did you! Well, don't that beat all?*** And he laughs, deep and reverberating, like lingering pulses of pleasure moments after the peak. ***Whatcha got in mind, little man?***

I tell him everything. I tell him my plan. I tell him what's at risk, and who. And I tell him what I'm offering.

He laughs even harder, and that's how I know he'll agree.

This branch is a ghost.

Their site has a board of directors and everything, completely proper for a non-profit. Except there's a problem with that: nobody on the board of directors exists. All the photos, names, and biographies are faked. More deniability, I think, and one heavily on my side when this goes to court.

I stare down the tree-lined street, eyeing the endgame. It's just a building; kind of ugly, square and gray with the barest hint of castellation along the top and largely empty apartment blocks flanking. It looks like an old armory, or just some fortified bank or something. Boring and imposing at once.

My heart's pounding in my throat. *Cassilda. Game on.*

*All recorded, all transmitted.*

*And when your network access is removed?*

*It won't be, boss. Analysis complete on the internal networks from the downed drone at the prison and the aggressive construct on the roof, and I have hacked into their main system.*

Ha! Gotta love my girl. I swear, there's no A.I. like her on the whole damn planet. *Good job. Make damn sure all of this goes on record.*

*You got it, boss.*

Time to get this show on the road.

Nothing to see here. Just an ordinary guy out for a walk, whistling to himself. Just a guy, out to take on a group of powerful connected tech-savvy racists.

The front gates are huge, like they mean for tanks to roll through there, or something. I look up—they're probably watching me from every angle—and I knock.

The sound of my knuckles goes precisely nowhere, of course, but it isn't about making a big noise. I did that by arriving.

Nothing happens. That's okay. We're all waiting to see what comes next, after all. I knock again: *shave-and-a-haircut.*

No bits.

That's okay. They're just trying to figure out my plan, because *obviously* I came with backup, with a bomb strapped to my heart, or some crazy shit. Right? I wouldn't do this without a plan. Nobody would do that.

Well, mine is currently to get their attention and hold it, and I'm good at doing that. *Knock, knock, knock-knock, knock.*

The construct's voice comes piping from above me somewhere, maybe above the doors. "This is an unexpected move, Mr. Night."

"Is it? That's funny. Here, I thought I was acting in character."

"Would you like to come in and speak face to face?" says the voice.

Here we go. Not that there's any actual escaping at this point; it's an illusion of freedom, and we both know it, but damn, the pull is strong. No running from this. Not if I want to end it. "Yeah, might as well. Make things a little easier, you know?"

"Indeed."

The gates part in the center along a perfect and invisible seam and swing open.

*Sixty-three attempts to hack me and counting.*

*Cassilda, protect yourself. If gathering data threatens your integrity, I want you to bail. Turtle mode.*

*Yes, boss.*

They won't break her. They've never seen anything like her.

So this isn't exactly what I expected for a bastion of so-called human purity and spooky-weird tech. I feel like I walked into a gods-damned Ren Faire. There's fucking *grass* halfway to my knees with thick, green blades and glistening dew. I'm on a dirt path, conspicuously dust-free and neatly edged. There's thick old trees with red fruit splashed all over, the kind you'd expect in a Fey garden—except in a Fey garden, it'd be genuinely wild, the magic shaping it as natural and gradual as the currents themselves.

Here, it's not so wild. Many humans like untamed beauty, but only in concept. In reality, they don't like the mess real trees make. They don't like how undergrowth smells, or that thorns draw blood; they don't like bugs, and squishy shit, and little tiny bodies left over from predation or just plain old age and illness. They especially don't like the fact that in the actual wild, there are things that can harm them.

So, they lock it all down and wrap it all up. Prune it all back and breed it all neat, scrape out natural soil to replace it with something prettier, kill anything they think is a threat, twist baby trunks to get the "wild" looks they want, trim inconvenient bare branches and asymmetrical leaves, and then wonder why the ecosystem keeps getting fucked.

This is that kind of beauty. It's not my thing, and more power to anybody who likes it, but the thing is... it's fake.

The sky? Is bright blue. It wasn't that outside, but more a gray cloud situation with that faint sparkle that comes from the People of the Sun's protections. This is not only illusion, but denial of reality outside. An interesting choice I'll have to analyze later.

Nobody's here, so I follow the path. I'm sure there are guns or drones with brain-fuck needles all trained on me, but if they were gonna go that route, I think they would have by now.

In front of me, in the middle of the path, the air shimmers. There's a door; the path looks like it continues, but it doesn't. I stop.

"We must admit, Mr. Night, that we did not initially put research into you," says the voice, which I think might belong to a woman, but who knows? "You were never the focus of this. We're willing to admit that you were involved completely by accident, which gives us some options."

"Yeah? That so?"

"Yes. Given your unplanned involvement, Mr. Night, we're ready to offer you an out—which is certainly more than you expected."

"Can't say I expected mercy, for sure." I lean into my Bahstonian. "Came here ta offah that ta *you* guys, actually."

The maybe-woman coughs lightly, like an aborted laugh. "Mr. Night, in all seriousness, what do you think *you* can offer *us?*"

"Well, here's what's on the table," I say. "I got definitive proof you people took out a prison and killed government employees. And I know, you prob'ly got your own shit, doctored, to make us look like we did it—but mine is unedited, and a little bit of work'll show that. More, you attacked the Crown Prince of the Silver Dawning, and even if he *is* on the outs, that'll make things precarious for you. Money speaks, and human governments don't like liabilities with trading partners. You'd find yourselves real expendable all of a sudden if this gets out."

"Money speaks—this is true," says the unimpressed maybe-woman. "So, you're blackmailing us? This is shaky reasoning. You may have a recording, but you're assuming anyone would ever see it. Is that actually all you brought?"

"Aw, come on, you gotta know that's not all I brought," I say. "And I'm not trying for blackmail. I'm trying for a trade."

"A trade," says the voice, coming from absolutely everywhere at once like she's trying to be a god.

"Yeah. Hey, you said face-to-face," I say. "Right now, it's face-to-invisible-door."

"So you *can* see it." The eagerness in that tone is, uh. Upsetting.

"Yeah?" I say.

"Your pupil sized changed, as did your heart rate. You can see through the protections we've put up—an interesting skill which we will have to study."

"Gonna crack my head open and see what's inside, are you?" I say, dry, trying to keep calm.

"No, not this time," she says regretfully.

Hoo, boy.

"Do you know what it is we do here?" she suddenly says.

Why would she ask me that? Does she want me to... understand? Is that it? Well, let's see if she's got pride to poke. "I know what you officially do. I know what you've been doing under the radar, too. Kids? Really? Are you trying to be the villains of your own damn history?"

Her voice gets tight, and suddenly she's having an argument I didn't start. "The history of medical advancement has never been bloodless. We, the future of the human race, are *not butchers*, and we do not view non-humans as subhuman. We value everyone we study, and provide as much dignity, where deserved, as we can. But testing must be done. Subjects are *necessary*. What we *are*, Mr. Night, is utterly ruthless in our pursuit of a means to protect ourselves from *you*."

Is she actually *monologuing*? "Seriously?"

"Very seriously, Mr. Night. We both know the only true power humanity has in the face of magic is that there are more of us."

She's not fully wrong. Even with how many people died during the mess before the Sun helped, they still outnumber us. Magical people—except for Kin—just don't reproduce quickly. Nobody's ever figured out why. "Sure, but I mean, ya gotta admit," I say, sticking my hands in my pockets, "if we were gonna hurt you the way you seem to fear, we'd have done it already. We wouldn't be waiting around. Nobody wants to enslave you or eat you or whatever it is you think is going on."

"Except, of course, for those who have been *enslaved* and *eaten* and *whatever is going on*," she snarls.

"Really? The exception proves the rule? So let's apply that logic. Let's take the outright murder your group just did, and assume that's how humans all behave to the rest of the Mythos for all time. How's that work out for you? You guys speared a human prison guard through the skull six hours ago because... what? No witnesses?"

There's the slightest pause. "A tidy argument, Mr. Night, with one problem: we kill when it is *necessary*. Your kind does so for pleasure."

"And serial killers don't count?"

"They do not. Aberrations are outliers and should not be counted."

Yeah, her critical reasoning is shot to hell. She can't see the parallels. Whatever. I ain't here for philosophical shit-takes. "Look, there's a door here, you don't know if I have what you want on me or not, and we both know the reason I'm not needle-brained already is you don't know why I walked in here and where the mirror is. Can we just get this over with?"

"Refreshingly brusque," she says. "I suppose whatever mixture you are, you don't have any Fey."

I laugh. Sorry, Grey, but it's true (and he'd probably gasp, put his hand over his heart, deny it, and then embody tomfoolery until nightfall). "Well, who can tell? I'm Kin. Nobody knows what I got in my blood."

"So you say." The door opens. It just appears, the light-based illusion falling away from it, and it simply slides out of sight into the "invisible" wall.

Here we go. Dagon better come through.

I walk inside.

Right, *this* looks like what I expected. While I know there's rich humans who embody the grandeur of "the olden days," of fictionalized lushness on every surface and sight, it's really the Fey and the Night Children who go all-in on the hedonism, which makes biased humans go the other way: anti-fabulous, white and sterile. Calmly lit, no eye-strain, ridiculously clean. White, white, white, so white I hate it, but I'm sure it pleases someone.

Ahead is a woman. Don't know her; her face ain't on the damn website, that's for sure. Her dark skin is soft and smooth, wrinkled with laugh-lines from happier times than this. She keeps her tight curls short, and wears no jewelry I can see beyond one bracelet that dangles below the cuff of her lab coat. The white she's wearing complements her skin; she doesn't look mean or cruel or hateful. She looks clever and tired; she looks like someone I'd like to have a drink with and see what kind of conversations we could have.

She looks me up and down. "You look so human. I'm never going to get used to that."

"Most Kin do. What, did you grow up on the moon?"

"Mars, actually," she says, which does explain a lot—only humans live there, or on the moon, and yeah, because what the hell does anybody even want with those places? Can't even go for a walk along the shore.

"Well, nice to meet you," I say, nodding. "Simon Night."

"Right," she says. "Doraleen Iskinder. Now. Do you have the Mirror?"

She says it capitalized, I swear to gods.

"Nope," I say. "Though—say it with me on script—*I know where it is.*"

Her lips twitch. She's got a sense of humor. I wonder if she wishes she could have a drink with me, too, in better times. "And since we're no longer beating around the bush, what, Mr. Night, do you want in return for it?"

"Real simple," I say. "I want you to leave Nate Scott the fuck alone."

Her smile—which shows around her eyes, deepening those laugh-lines—fades. "That's curious."

"Is it, though?" I raise one eyebrow.

"Yes. He's your business rival. We have recordings of the two of you having fist-fights in public places."

"Hey, only a couple," I say, genial. "And we got that all worked out. That was years ago."

"Still. You have only one competitor; one would think losing your rival would be a boon, if anything."

She's pushing back, and by doing so, confirmed this whole shebang was somehow a sting for him, even if the mirror is part of the deal. "I ain't budging, ma'am. Leave Scott out of this, and I'll tell you where the mirror is."

"That's a very small request for such a valuable artifact," she says, fishing for clues, deflecting my demand.

"Is it, though?"

"Yes. What do you think to gain?"

"I think it's more what *you* think you can get out of him that you can't get out of anybody else," I say.

She pauses. Frowns. Maybe she's listening to her own AI assistant, I dunno. "That's... a rational question," she says. "I'll answer it. As I said, dignity where deserved. The problem, Mr. Night, is that his heritage is traceable, and yours is not."

Wow. Okay. Wow. That is some information I did *not* have. "You know his heritage?"

"And yours, to four generations back," she says.

That's more than I ever heard. Even he only knew his mother. "Lady, we were both orphans. He just lucked out by inheriting wealth."

"DNA doesn't lie," she says.

"Wh... you've had *both* our DNA long enough to trace that?" I say, really lost now. "The fuck for?"

"Mr. Night..." She hesitates.

Oh, please monologue. Come on, lady, do it. Do it. "Yeah? Come on, what are you going around collecting random DNA for?"

"It. Isn't. Random." She bites off the words like I insulted her intelligence. "You two are among the most unique, human-passing Kin in the city, and we know his provenance," she says like he's a fine wine. "It only made sense to start with him."

I speak slowly. "For... what?"

She sighs. "Do you know *frustrating* it is, Mr. Night?"

Sounds like a monologue introduction! "No, ma'am. Why don't you tell me?"

"It's frustrating that a single disease with hardly any variation could wipe our People out," she snaps, and walks toward me. "It's frustrating that no disease we've yet been able to discover or manufacture can affect the Darkness, or the Sun. Frustrating that the Guardians' very nature burns out any illness, that the Dream is somehow *phased* enough that they're barely physical, that the Fey have such keen control over their magic that they can simply remove infection with laser-like precision, and that the Kin—closest to us, born from us, stealing our mortality and our ability to breed in exchange for *nothing*—are so disparate and so varied that no disease seems able to take hold of more than a handful of them, either, though it should be possible!"

The hell. I stare at her.

She stops walking about a meter from me. Exhales slowly, visibly seeking calm. "Mr. Night. We are not insane. We are not murderers, or perpetrators of genocide. We don't want to kill all of you. We just want the means to protect ourselves, and step one must be *early detection.*"

"I think you might've switched tracks there a little bit," I say carefully, because she just jumped from biowarfare to some kinda privacy invasion, all while saying she's not nuts, and I suddenly find myself wondering when the last time was she had a conversation with another person who wasn't ass-deep in all this.

"Not really. Kin rarely die from disease; they survive plague-ridden areas and horrifying flu, which is why they spread their mutated genes and further pollute our genetic code. They can't catch that plague, but they can, Mr. Night, be *carriers.* Your existence threatens us."

That seems a *little* broad. "Our existence?"

"Your entire *existence*, because you walk among us, because you aren't easily detected, because for most of human history, you've strutted around, spreading illness you yourselves cannot feel, ending human lives before they have a chance to reproduce, while spreading your own ruined genetic code. Am I making things clear here, Mr. Night?" She takes a deep breath. "I'm off-topic. I know we've had a difficult introduction, but we are willing to put all that aside—though not for the cost mentioned. You are allowed to leave if you give us what we want."

My voice is strained. "I thought you were gonna crack my head open."

"Only if you volunteered. We aren't *murderers.* We don't need your head now. Give us the Mirror, and you can return to your life. We do need Mr. Scott's body, I'm afraid, and there is no negotiating that point—but you can go."

They need—

I swallow. I'm sure they're measuring my heart rate, my pupil-size, my rising temperature, but I can't control those things. They need his body? They need his fucking *body?*

They're going to kill him no matter what?

Well. Well, that settles it then, don't it? Plan B with the nuclear option, and damn the consequences for me. "You think I'm gonna believe that?" I say. "That you'd just let me go?"

"I think you'd be a fool not to. We have no reason to kill you. Your heritage is largely unknown, and therefore useless. Besides, everyone knows you're Kin. It's not like you're one of the Cuckoo's false eggs, waiting to push contenders out of the nest."

I know there are weapons pointed at me. Any second, and she could lose patience, give the order, take me out, but I can't quit now. I *push*. "Why do you need his body?"

"As I explained, because of his heritage. He's from very important stock, Mr. Night—unique, without exaggeration. He's a perfect control subject."

"For making couture *disease?*"

She sighs like she'd hoped I'd get it, like she'd had high expectations for her new Kin pupil, but I disappointed her in the end. "For protecting ourselves against future outbreaks. Where is the Mirror, Mr. Night? I won't ask you again."

And I'm sure she won't. After this, they'll just drug me and try for info the hard way, dignity not deserved. I sigh, too. "So. Here's the thing. You're talkin' about the Peoples, and especially Kin, like maybe you think with a little more time, you can understand how *all* the magical Peoples work, and maybe figure out how to infect all the folks you think are too scary. But in all that talk, I never heard you mention gods."

Her look is so dry. It's the best *Teacher Detecting Bullshit* expression I have ever seen. "Why would I mention mythology, Mr. Night?"

Oh, you're about to *learn*. "Well," I say, scratching the back of my head where a needle is probably just aching to go, "one of them has your mirror."

She sighs again, looking weary as hell. "I swear, if you've sent us on a goose chase... it took *years* to track down the first time. What supposed 'god' has it, then?"

My turn to deflect. "What do you want it for, anyway? You don't use magical gewgaws."

"We're going to reverse engineer it and see how it really works. Magic isn't a thing, Mr. Night. It's manipulation of scientific principles. With the proper tools, humans can do all the same tricks."

She's wrong. She's so wrong. A scientific achievement can mimic magic, but it is not and never will be the same. "'Supposed' god?"

"Really? We... fine. There are no gods. That very concept is a religious paleologism. There are beings, both with a concept of personhood and without, naturally gifted with certain levels of ability, as well as strengths and weaknesses. Whoever you gave it to is no more a god than you are, Mr. Night."

I can't let them kill Scott. I can't. So. Time to trigger the mess. "Oh, I ain't a god." I wipe sweat from hairline onto my fingers. It didn't have to be sweat; could be any bodily fluid, but this, born of stress and not heat, is both convenient and appropriate. "I was conceived the normal way, of flesh and blood and magic. I'll die—maybe here, the way things are going—and my soul will leave, and my body will rot, even if you study it, going back to feed the Earth that made it. But, uh. Ma'am. No offense. You're wrong about gods. They weren't born. They don't die. And they sure as hell don't rot."

I rub my fingers together. Sweat, filled with salt and nerves and desperation, touches the borrowed blue ring on my index finger, and the ring's subtle waves begin to dissolve.

Gods like Dagon don't usually get too directly involved. It's not worth it to them; all our trials and travails are a single blink of time. Nothing worth fretting about. That not-here-ness is *why* people like Doraleen can doubt them with such ease; can't see, can't catch, can't test or observe or measure.

Don't mean they're not around.

The magic ring on my finger dissolves to salty, swirling liquid and falls from my finger to the pristine white floor, and though I can't hear it land, it just rang in the undercity like a damn dinner bell.

"Have it your way," she says, like my own little monologue was just spitting in her face.

And I don't know what her people hit me with; barely felt it, in the back of my neck, but whatever it is stings and spreads real fast. They didn't aim for my head, because after all, they need me alive, because after all, there's no guarantee my Kin brain would hang around like a human one for them to extract information, because after all, they had time to study me and boy *howdy* I don't know what they used but I feel like I just got kicked by an elephant, and I go down.

It was an effective cocktail. But it wasn't quite strong enough.

I'm aware of... *sounds* like nobody's business, of shaking floors and cracking walls (or maybe that's just my bones), of Doraleen's shouted commands and shrieking escape, and Dagon's laugh flooding the place even as it *is* flooded by him and his children (so damn *many* in Boston, and lady, you want Kin, I'll fucking *give you so many Kin* you won't even know what's a banana), and maybe there's music, because it's a party, you know, that's what I started, because someone like Dagon has seen people come and go and cults rise and fall and what does *he* care about shit like this, except I promised a hell of a party, and a prize for Gany, and more'n that, I promised to be here.

And I promised to sing.

I never claimed to be a singer. I mean. I *can* do it. No Fey in me, so it isn't that kind of magic. What I do have? Is the Sun. Their music is the jaw-ful tone of pure-rung bells and steady light, the playful dance of flickering heat and wind-kissed smoke. So when someone like Grey sings, they make magic. When someone like I sings... when... me sings... me... I can make *feeling*. Atmosphere. Warmth. And that works real good for what I promised Dagon.

Dagon gets a pass as a god because he at least cares about his offspring, and for what he is, he ain't a bad guy. Still. Don't ever sing for a god, kids. Like some damn toddler, they remember, and always ask for *more*.

The cold salt-water cure that rushes through my veins has to be his power, and it's a perfect antidote to whatever the Association pumped into me, but I don't like it, and it's the opposite of everything I am, even if it is a good fix.

Not enough of a fix, though. I'm still out of it, so out of it, hallucinating, and all I can see is wild colors and glorious sky and ocean stretching forever, even though I *know* we're in a blocky gray building near Corey Hill.

***You should make some music, little man,*** says the god who holds me like a doll, and though my lungs are filled with rain and my eyes are filled with fire, somehow, through the steam, I sing.

# CHAPTER 10

## SPOUSAL PERMISSIONS

literally steamed up the place. Time didn't matter for this party, days of water and heat and music and laughter (and tears because I missed my husband but they respected that while I was singing so nobody *touched* me), and then...

Look, I don't actually remember most of what happened. I got told, and I saw the aftermath. The news for the next six months dramatized the *illegal operations* discovered right in the heart of Boston, with footage of outright confession from a disgraced scientist and a facility belonging to some lunatics "gone rogue" who'd kidnapped Kin children to experiment on them.

Told you. Deniability.

And who got to be the headliner through all of that, the hero through the investigation and deliberation and exhumation and mess? Ganymede, of course.

It was Gany's time to shine (literally) in the sun. I made sure all the footage Cassilda took seemed to come from him, which meant some careful editing, but she's good, real good, and all the collected evidence backed him up, so nobody looked too close.

Funny enough, though I've worked with him for nearly ten years, it's the first time I've ever seen him aboveground. He's fuckin' gorgeous? Looks like some kinda nymph or something, blue skin and delicate fins poking out from his silky blue hair, and a shy look with big eyelashes that lets folks ignore the fucking shark teeth peeking behind those full, blue lips.

I mean, *I* know he's basically sentient water, and his *family* knows he's basically sentient water, but the media don't need to know that.

Anyway. Story goes, his little brother went missing, and no one would listen, so he went on his own search, and busted this nightmare-operation wide open.

Current scuttlebutt claims Kin were being stolen to harvest their organs for... something. That rumor'll change soon enough. Point is, Gany's a hero (which Dagon wanted) and getting his fifteen minutes of fame, and he sent me a grainy photo of himself looking *real* happy wrapped around some other individual of vaguely human proportions with the line, *I said yes.*

Good for him.

You know who else said yes? Me, once upon a time, and when I finally wake after the party (which mysteriously lasted three days, and also went unremarked by any authority or surveillance), I am soaked to the bone, lying in the dark in the undercity, and so tired I can barely think.

*Welcome back, boss.*

*Thanks, Cassilda.*

I just stagger home.

There are three envelopes outside my door—which, wow, that's expensive. The hell?

One holds an invitation to the wedding of the Prince of the Silver Dawning John Barron McCarrig and... hm. The other name is something I can neither hear *nor* read, apparently.

The second envelope holds a cancellation for the wedding of the Prince of the Silver Dawning John Barron McCarrig and whoever. Good for you, Grey.

The third holds a *hefty* credit stone with three times my daily rate on it, and a note from Grey himself: *Thanks.*

You're welcome, kid.

Right. Time to take my medicine. I open the door.

My husband is waiting for me.

My husband is *pissed.*

Scott grabs me the moment I walk in, pushing me up against the wall like he wants to start another fight, and squeezing nasty water from my shirt through his fists as he yells right in my face. "What were you *thinking?*"

"They were going after you," I tell him, too tired to do a proper fight, even though we both like 'em. "You, specifically. I had to stop them."

He just stares at me. Then he breaks down crying, and that feels worse, way worse, *so much worse* than anything else that's gone on this week.

We sink to the floor, and I'm sopping wet and tired, but he's pale and wide-eyed because he thought I was dead, and I needed him to not *be* dead, and fuck, what a pair we make.

"I'm sorry," I say, holding him, and I don't know who's rocking who, I don't know who's crying harder, I don't know what's what anymore, except that at least with me being so wet, our tears blend. "I'm sorry. I couldn't let them."

"You *tell me* next time. I thought... you *jerk*," Scott says weakly, and I laugh weakly, and we resume where we left off.

The world can go to hell. Is the Association after us? I don't know. Is human authority? I don't know. Gany said they're not, that enough of Dagon's people work in government to make it all go away. I have to trust him. *Cassilda,* I tell her. *Lock us in. Fucking honeymoon protocol time.*

*You've got it, boss,* she says, securing our home, auto-programming meals so we don't have to go anywhere, blocking all the news, starting our enormous bath up with bubbles and scents, and turning on the nice colored lights in our bedroom with soft, voiceless music as if we need any help knowing where to go.

Honeymoon mode stays active for ten days, and we take every second of those ten. We talk. A lot. I apologize for leaving him in the dark. He apologizes for not telling me what I was getting into. We work it all out.

And we remember why we got married, because rivals or not, there's nobody like us for knowing each other, and understanding each other, and wrenching the best kind of cries from each other, and the world, like I said, can go right to hell.

So all of that's why we didn't hear the news about who came to town until the guy knocked on our front door, all our joint protections be damned.

*Knock, knock.*

I lift my head like some kinda Muppet. "Fuck?" I query.

Scott ignores it.

*Knock, knock.*

"Uh," I say, too bleary to think clearly. "Cassilda? Who's out there?"

*Kfshssh gb it lvshsh agbr shh, boss.*

*Cassilda?*

Static. Just static.

Oh. Um. That's. Fiiiine.

What could do that? What in *fuck* could do that? My heart feels tight. "Stay," I murmur to Scott (who's worn out right now, yes, he *is*, thank you very much), throw on a robe, run my hand through my bird's-nest hair, and head to the door.

Whoever got past our wards without us feeling a thing has got to be... big. I don't got a weapon that'd hurt someone that big, so my grand plan is non-confrontation and hoping this isn't something bad. Not now. We just won. Let us have this, universe. Come on.

Tech's not working. Magic fizzles out. Even the peephole shows nothing but a swirling, feathery black.

Nothing else to do. I open the door.

A guy stands there. Stunningly handsome in that particular way that you just know he's a romantic fiend: cut jaw, black hair, blue eyes, scruff that looks designer—an absolute retro movie-pirate vibe. And as he smiles, the raw weight of his power presses into me, and I know who he is.

I'd know him if I passed him on the street. I'd know him behind a brick wall, and that means he was hiding himself until I opened the door to ensure I didn't run, which is smart because I have the absolutely fuck-mad urge to turn, grab my husband, and dive out the back window.

Running makes the predators chase you. "Please don't have broken my assistant," I say to Bran, the Darkseed, the Raven King, the lord of Umbra and all the People of the Darkness.

"It's temporary," he says, the burr of his accent absolutely as magnificent as imagined, and we both pretend his true form isn't a seven-foot-tall devil with cracked skin the color of burned brick and light flickering through those cracks as if from far away. "No recording this," he says.

Cassilda. "Better be temporary," I say, rough.

He looks amused. "May I come in?"

The Raven King just possibly fried my A.I., and then asked permission to come into my home. "What happens if I say no?"

He looks like he hadn't considered that. "I hadn't considered that," he says. "Well, if you do, that's fine, but I'd hate to talk to him without you there. Not that I'm married, but I understand. One flesh, and all that."

He's. Ridiculously charming?

Those words should have been threatening. They're not. Delivered with such affability, such light humor, that you know he's actually making fun of the thing that might upset you. But *what* he said didn't escape me. "You got *any* idea what happened last week?"

"Some," he says, which could mean anything.

"I'm not letting you talk to my husband," I say, nice and calmly. "And if that means I have to get Xu Kai himself involved in this mess—"

"Whoa, now," he says, low and easy, hands up. "I'm not here to threaten anyone. You've got my word, three times if you need it."

I stare. "You normally go around giving magical oaths to nobodies?"

"When they're family," he says, and the penny drops, and before I can say another word, Scott's behind me.

Warm. Solid. Steady where I shake, wobbly where I'm strong. Standing there like he's not facing threat all over. "So you came," he says.

What? What?

"You expected me?" says the Raven King.

"Hold on," I snap. "What?"

They are both quiet for a moment, these two men, and suddenly, I see it. Scott is blond and the Raven King is dark, and Scott's beard is neat and the Raven King has stubble, but it's there. Resemblance. My husband's not a shape-shifter, but there's a clear inheritance of human guise, however Darkness genetics work. Even if Doraleen hadn't laid the groundwork, I'd know.

Fuck. I turn and look at Scott, who's gone pale.

He takes a slow breath, in and out, controlled. "Among the Mythos," he starts.

"The fuck is happening right now?" I verbalize.

"Formalities matter," Scott says, because for people like him, they do. "They help us maintain diplomacy, preventing the shedding of blood." And then he slides his arm around my waist and looks at Bran over my shoulder as if to stake a claim. Or maybe as if to say, *Hey, however you feel about things, this is an **us**. Take it or leave it.*

Fuck, I love this idiot. I'm so scared for him.

"Among the Mythos, I am Kin, called Nate Scott," Scott continues. "This is my husband, also Kin, called Simon Night."

"Well and well met!" says the intruder effusively. "Among the Mythos, I am Darkness, of the Shadow's Breath, called Bran."

This cannot be happening. "Just Bran? We're all just folks now, having a chat?"

"I think if he'd come with intent to harm, we'd be harmed," says Scott with more grace than I've ever had, in spite of the tremor in his voice. "Come in. Sit down. Drink coffee. Leave as you came: in peace."

"To this, I agree. Be well. Be whole. I will leave you as I found you: in peace." And Bran walks by us, dwarfing us both.

Is he taking my husband away? What's happening here? "Seriously? I didn't realize by 'formal,' you meant 'pre-Industrial Revolution,'" I mutter at them.

"Adorable," says Bran, dry.

And though I didn't think that was an insult, Scott responds. "That's strike one. You only get one more."

Bran stops in the entryway to our kitchen and looks back at us. Shadows fill the space between his cheekbones and furrowed brow. "Really serious with him, is it?"

"Yes. Coffee, please," says Scott, who just defended me though I don't need it.

This idiot. This wonderful, endangered idiot. "I can stand up for myself," I tell him.

"Yes. Coffee, please," says Scott, in his calm and soothing way—the way he gets perps talking, just as much as my plate-smashing.

He's still shaking, though. So am I as I make the damn coffee. *Cassilda, tell me you're okay. Please.*

*Unable to record, boss,* she says, because she's incredible, and she figured a way around the Raven King's assault.

I lean on the counter for a moment, head down. I could cry with relief. *What happened?*

*My system took in too much data. A re-routing was necessary to resume processing. I cannot access it without further unresponsiveness on my part. Otherwise, boss, I am well.*

Better be. Better *fucking* be, or I'm punching his Raven dick.

No recording, but I get Cassilda back. Okay. It's a step in the right direction. We can do this, whatever it is.

Behind me, the love of my life and my latest nightmare sit across from each other at our tiny kitchen table. "So you're not surprised I'm here," Bran says, resuming the doorway conversation.

"I expected you years ago."

"Did you?"

"Before my mother died, she warned me. I was terrified of your coming, in fact."

Bran's face tightens. "What happened to her?"

"Do you really care?" says Scott in an utterly non-confrontational tone.

"Yes," says Bran. "I liked her."

I put Scott's coffee mug in front of him, and he looks down into it as he answers. "She died in the Woburn explosion."

Bran winces.

Yeah, that was a great big mess. Natural gas harvesting, no regulations followed, kaboom. Killed a lot of people.

I put Bran's coffee down (in our ugliest green mug with the brown pattern that looks like poop). Then I sit just a little apart so they can keep talking.

"That was a tragedy," Bran says.

"You're not here to talk about human tragedy," says Scott.

"No." Bran sips. "Technically, you're the Crow King, so I reckon we should talk about that."

"The *fuck?*" I say.

Scott chokes a little, politely coughing behind his napkin. "Excuse me?"

"Though naturally, we need to test that hypothesis first," says Bran, and places that damned mirror shard on the table.

I slam a dish towel over it. The towel has happy dancing T-rexes, kind of killing the dramatic effect, but whatever. Don't care. "How the fuck did you *get* this?"

"When you give something to a god, it's good to remember that they don't always... value those things the way you do," says Bran gently.

Son of a bitch. "Fuck that fish-fucking asshole!"

"It's all right!" says Bran, as if it could be. "It's safe now."

Maybe he really isn't here to do harm. And maybe I can fly and just never figured it out. "What, with you?"

Scott puts his hand over mine, then looks back and forth between us, lowering the napkin. "Shouldn't you return it to the Lins? They'd hired me to bring it undercover to a second bank of theirs after the first was broken into. At least theoretically, they wanted to safeguard it."

Bran looks grim. "I think they're better off if it stays gone. They didn't want it in the first place, and whoever the spy is over there—"

"Because the spy can't possibly be someone of yours," I snap.

"No. It can't," he says far too mildly to be safe for anyone who works for him. "Whoever it is might act again. I won't risk this falling into the wrong hands."

Eleanore Lin said their debt was paid (and I will be kicking over *that* kettle later). What else is the Association into? What if the debt goes back to being not paid? What if there's more leverage? Damn it, he's right; the mirror can't go back to them, but I don't have to like it. "And I suppose your hands are the right ones."

"For now," he says.

Scott rubs his chin. "Okay. Okay, that... we'll get into all that later. How does it work?"

"Magic," says Bran with an absolute *brat* grin.

Scott just looks at him.

"Great!" I say. "Now that's solved, take it away, thank you."

"Sorry, but no," Bran says, though he isn't. "It works by connection through time itself. The reason it can't be remade is it's made from a piece of Chronos."

I stare at him. "Sure."

Scott frowns. "Chronos? The before-god? The source of time?"

"His blood, specifically, when Dis, his daughter, killed him," says Bran like any of this is believable or makes sense or is real (but is it *that* much of a stretch?), and points to the dish towel. "It echoes. Echoes backwards through your genes to the combination of organic and magic that made *you*, to the combination of organic and magic that made *them*, and so forth. In the process, if your forebears are alive, they'll see through the connection, or tunnel, that bit of time dilation made."

I believe him. Gods help me, I believe him. "That's what it does, not how," I challenge.

"What you're really asking me is if it will harm him," says Bran.

And he's right, but I hate the way he went there. Kingly. We're gonna clash a lot if he hangs around, I can already tell. "Yeah."

"If he were weak, you'd need to be concerned," says Bran. "But he isn't. He tested Garnet. He'll be fine."

Shit.

"Why would we need to be concerned otherwise?" Scott says.

"Ah. With really weak Kin, the minimal magic they have gets... unwoven? At least, according to old records. They cease to exist, fall outside of time, maybe out of existence. It's why this thing was hidden away, in the end."

"And you want to use it on *him?*" I blurt.

"It won't hurt him, but I have to be sure."

"No, you don't," I say. "The Association already knew, confirmed. You can use whatever fuckin' proof *they* have."

Bran stares at me. That... oh, holy hell. That look is *thunder*. That look is catastrophe, the shadow of a seismic wave, the smell and crack of a house already on fire. "Did they, now? How intriguing," he says so quietly.

Beings like Bran don't play in the same pool we do. They're not gods, but we come nowhere near the kind of power they wield. I got a feeling Bran is gonna be doing some investigating of his own, and I don't think they're gonna like how that plays out.

Might spur them toward *magical beings must die.* Might make them re-think everything. Don't know yet.

"Well," Bran says. "I'm afraid that makes it even more important. If you're under my protection, no one will dare come after either of you. But if you're not, and it's known you're my rejected offspring, you're fucked."

He's right. *Again.* I got what I could out of Gany. It's wild that Dagon helped as much as he did. Bran is right: we need his protection.

"I see," says Scott, low. "Give us a minute. Night and I need to talk."

"I'll wait here," says the Raven King cheerily, and snaps his fingers. A sound barrier apparently goes up, though it's above my pay grade and I can't see it. He grins and starts singing Gilbert and Sullivan's "A British Tar," if my lip-reading's any good, but we don't hear a peep.

Show-off.

Scott pulls me back, into our bedroom, and closes the door. There, he presses me into the wall, leaning in, and breathing deeply against my neck.

I breathe deeply myself, stroking his back, feeling every familiar bumpy vertebrae. "So."

"So." He takes another deep breath. "That's my father."

"I picked up on that." I swallow. "You told me you didn't know him."

"I don't. I've never seen him before today." Scott's still shaking. "I'm sorry. I should've told you this."

"Yeah."

"I know this is maybe a step too far. This is what you *don't* want. This kind of connection, pushing us into the spotlight. We talked about this before—"

"Not about *this*," I drawl. "Sure as hell never mentioned your paternity problem."

"I'm sorry."

It's funny, the lies we tell ourselves. The secrets we keep, thinking we'll lose the love we accidentally stumbled into one day like tripping over a cache of treasure. I hid shit, trying to protect him. He hid shit, trying to keep me. You know... I think it evens out, and I think it gives us a path forward. I stroke down his spine some more, familiar and calming for us both. "Me, too. Guess this balances out me running around doing crazy shit behind your back, huh?"

"It didn't *need* balancing. I don't know what to do."

"Yeah, you do."

He scoffs. "I'm not going to be a king."

"King Investigations has a ring to it, though. I could make my new name Knight with a K, and then we'd be—"

He kisses me. So we just do that for a minute.

"If you need to leave, I won't stop you," he says.

*That* gets an eyeroll. "As if I'd leave you for something you got no control over?"

"You're handling this awfully well," he says.

My turn for a dry look. "Make you a deal. You tell me everything about your mom—what she taught you, all the shit you hid—and I'll stick by your royal ass as you become a crow, or whatever the hell happens next. Sound good?"

He manages a bittersweet smile. "We were going to do that anyway."

"Even better, then," I say, deadpan, as if I only just thought of it. "Quick. Better take the deal before your spouse figures out you're getting the better end."

He laughs again and kisses again, gripping my hair as if to keep both our heads above water. "You're sure?" he finally whispers.

"Yeah."

"Then let's go find out what it means to be a Crow King."

He does something then he never does—laces his fingers with mine as we walk back to our tiny kitchen side by side, equals, rivals, and inseparable.

Bran smiles and lowers his barrier.

Dunno how this is gonna go. Dunno how we're gonna make it through. But *we will.* Eyes wide open. Magic ready. Minds sharp. After all... I *gotta* know what happens next.

# NOTTE'S BOOK OF KNOWLEDGE

In the time before time, the First War ended the peace of the Peoples of the Earth. Driven and desperate, survivors bred for power and magic, and they succeeded—with a legacy too great for their mortal forms, and a homeworld they left in pieces.

Afraid, they turned to Naktam, the Lord of Night Whispers, oldest of them all, and begged for advice—for he was strangest, and the most resilient. He knew Death by name, and embodied the hunger of all worlds; thus it was he taught them to define by families, to use soul's desire and blood's prime powerto join those like themselves.

The Seven Peoples of the Earth—the Sun, the Darkness, the Guardians, the Fey, the Dream, the Kin, and the Ever-Dying who have no magic—came to find their own through blood and spirit, and choose the symbols to rally by. In time, simpler symbols were added for the sake of time and varying skill.

Today, the Seven Peoples remain strong, balanced, and free, and few there are who fight this many-reined yoke.

## THE SUN

**Hunger**: Hhealing.

**Prime power**: Light and heat.

**Homeworld**: Zenith, which is very hot, has numerous major stars, and is clean, regimented, and always welcomes those who are sick and require succor.

The People of the Sun bred for fire, light, qne heat, as a means to burn away infection and evil. This power grows over time; toward the end of their natural lifespan, their physical forms can no longer take the strain of magic coursing through them, and those who are the most ancient and venerated grow hotter, and hotter, and eventually explode into ash.

# THE DARKNESS

**Hunger**: Hunger itself.

**Prime power:** Darkness.

**Homeworld**: Umbra, in which is no light at all—it *cannot* be perceived or felt in that place, except in small pockets which its Lord may design.

Those who are of the Darkness *hunger*. Most eat; some collect. There are those who can and do devour anything, including plague, radiation, and the dead. The Fey, in particular, are much prized, their magic unique for whatever the Throne and Scepter do to it before sending it back out.

Toward the end of their natural lifespan, their own forms can no longer satisfy their aching, empty need. Those who are the most ancient and venerated grow more shadowed, less substantial, and eventually fade like mist in morning sun..

# THE GUARDIANS

**Hunger**: Protection.

**Prime power**: Resistance.

**World**: Officially, none.

Guardians are driven to protect. This need can attach itself to anything; there are sphinxes still guarding tombs deep underground, where they will remain until they die.

Something terrible happened in the First War, and those Guardians who remain are uniformly mad. Most still function amoing the Peoples, but rumors say the most powerful are locked away for the safety of all.

The Guardians are wildly varied in terms of natural lifespan. Some fairies live months; dragsons can live for centuries. The Saqalu, who inspired the four-winged symbol of the People of the Guardians, did not age.

However, no one lives forever; the Saqalu are gone, now called the Hashritu, the Broken, and are lost to all but memory.

# THE FEY

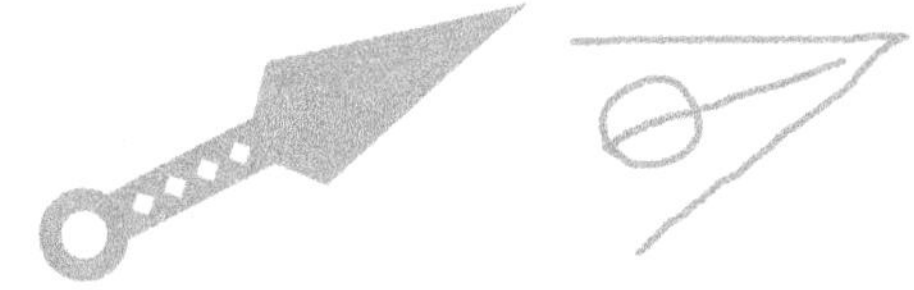

**Hunger**: Curiosity.

**Prime power**: Creation.

**World**: The Silver Dawning, divided between the Seelie Scepter and Unseelie Throne.

The Fey, flighty and mercurial, often discover and build only to abandon. They are in part driven by an unnatural need to reclaim the magic stolen from them; all their power, from birth, is channeled until the Throne and Scepter, there to be distributed and wielded as needed to keep their People alive. Mostly, though, the Fey are driven by curiosity. *Can I make it work?* is eye-rollingly funny as a trope.

Alone among the Seven Peoples, the Fey must seek magic outside of themselves, or starve; it is a skill learned to weave it from others, from emotion or intimacy, from applause or anguish. Toward the end of their natural lifespan, they lose the ability to process these stolen strands of power. Their bodies grow cool, and still; they become smooth, pale stone, without blemish, and without life. When Fey reach the natural end of their lives, they leave behind them soulless statues of themselves, echoes of the beauty they once held.

# THE DREAM

**Hunger**: Dreams.

**Prime power:** The influence and digestion of the unconscious mind.

**World**: The Plane of Dreams, guarded by ambulant trees, home to complete silence.

The Dream are rarely seen. They withrew from the horrors of the First War, and now dwell between realms, living in the walls that divide wake and sleep. Some taste nightmares and build them to madness; some share sweetness and encourage hope.

Their lifespans are unknown. The end of their natural existence is unknown. Inheritors of uneasy flesh, they have lost the ability to manifest sharply in our world for more than moments of time, and it remains unclear if they can ever rejoin those who truly live.

# THE KIN

**Hunger**: Varied.

**Prime power**: Varied.

**World**: All worlds, but primarily the human Earth.

The majority of Kin appear human, and are the source of all tales of humans who wield such power. They aren't one thing or another, neither fish nor flesh nor good red herring, but the legacy of many Peoples, who nevertheless rarely recognize Kin as their own. Due to unpredictable genetics, Kin powers vary wildly.

The Kin were once trafficked. They themselves could be used to increase the numbers of an identifiable People progeny, and so Kin were taken, used, and discardded—until nine brave families stepped forward to claim the Kin's place upon the Great Wheel. Lin, Blackwood, Lester, Sims, Doe, Yang, Bard, Roth, and Williams: may their names never be forgotten! Those who had no home now do, a People and a power and presence to be respected.

# THE EVER-DYING

**Hunger**: Discovery.

**Prime power**: None.

**World**: Earth.

From the viewpoint of the magical among the Mythos, humans are dying from the moment they're born. They are horrifyingly short-lived. Anything can kill them; worse tet, they have no magic, and can neither wield nor perceive its use.

They can, however, reproduce at a rate rarely seen outside of rabbits.

Notte, Naktam who chose the Peoples, the Lord of the Night Whispers, regards the Ever-Dying as precious, for only they can become his children. His intervention and protection enabled their growth, and ensured their place on the Wheel even though they have no magic.

# THE LOST

**Hunger**: Unknown.

**Prime power**: Terrible.

**World**: Unknown.

"Lost" is a misnomer. Tthe Scepter and the Fey saw that many did not fit into the sillos of the Seven Peoples of the Earth, and so tried to claim them. After all, their magic could continue to power the Silver Dawning.

This turned out to be a bad idea. Some beings could be claimed, yes, and their magic stolen, but the rest...

Gods. Demons. Psychopomps. Those things which eschew names and descriptions as worthless and ill-fitted. Many live outside of reality in the Void; too, are those who are not native to Earth, even as it was before it shattered. Of these, less said is better said. They are frightening, for none know what drives them.

# AMONG THE MYTHOS, WHO ARE YOU?

No one is defined by their People, any more than an ethnicity or culture determines who a person is, but it does influence environment and options. Understanding this ancient rubric is the first step into this world, and explains why these beings always introduce themselves thus: **Among the Mythos, I am [People,] called [name.] Who are you?**

# LEXICON

## IN WHICH IS LISTED NAMES AND TERMS

## CHARACTERS

**Bran**: Prince of the People of the Darkness. Of the Shadow's Breath, he is powerful and beautiful—though for *some* reason, he prefers appearing in his human guise instead of as his enormous, seven-foot-tall, horned, brick-red self.

**Cassilda:** An artificial intelligence, designated Personal Assistant category. Highly adaptive, she's Simon Night's favorite helper. There are many such Small Language Models, technically, but none are quite like Simon's. There is a reason for that...

**Dagon:** Dagon is, to put it bluntly, a god. From the Void, he's an ocean-dwelling being with the patience of ancient depths and a dry, wry sense of humor. He also has a tendency to make half-god offspring; there are a lot of Kin who don't know it, but they're of Dagon's line. He brought a lot of strange aquatic beings with him when he crossed over, not native to Earth. He's easy-going, but wants what he wants, and as a god, usually gets it. What he wants, usually, is just a good time (hence enjoying Simon Night singing for him), and is one of the only gods who's stepped out of the Void regularly onto Earth.

**Doraden Iskinder:** Doraleen is one of many truly brilliant people from the Iskinder family. Her great grandparents fled South Africa during the ecological disaster that led to the Sun needing to save the planet, and unfortunately, fell under the sway of the Association while living on Mars. Doraleen is a complicated person. She truly only wants to protect humans from Kinborn diseases; but she also turns a blind eye to the members of the Association who want to destroy Kin, seeing their very existence a danger.

**Eleanor Lin:** Matriarch of the Lin family, she is a stern lady, entirely devoted to tradition and the importance of appearances. She holds the reputation of her family in an iron grip, and though all her dealings could not be called above-board, none of them are done without a heavy level of introspection and risk assessment.

**Ganymede Galene:** Offspring of Dagon, high priest of the Boston Undersea, One With the Water, Master of the Damp Portal between this place and the multi-dimensional wonder of the oceans, he is a nerd who loves cards and collectibles, and has almost no self-confidence.

**Grey:** John Barron Grey, né McCarrig: Son of Owen McCarrig, son of Leith of the Stone, son of Eithne the Offspring of Stars, daughter of Mab. Grey is a runaway Unseelie prince and heir to The Throne. Kind of a brat. Fortunately for him, he's endearing.

**Jack Baptiste:** A Night-Child, owner of a bar in Boston. He's a reserved, quiet man with connections absolutely everywhere. His word is good for anything, and he always pays his debts. Of course, he always collects them, too.

**Lin Family:** One of the nine most powerful families of the Kin, famous for their fight to earn recognition for Kin as a full People, wealthy through generations of smart deals... and some not so smart ones. Their current matriarch is Eleanore, Katie Lin's mother.

**Natural Scott:** One of two licensed Kin detectives in Boston, Nate Scott is clever, dangerous, and elegant. Of the Kin, specifically Ever-Dying and the Darkness, he was orphaned young, is wealthy by inheritance, and happens to be utterly charming. To everyone's surprise, he is also the Darkseed, son of Bran. He's married to Simon Night, and wouldn't have it any other way.

**Simon Night:** One of two licensed private investigators in Boston, Simon is tough, no-nonsense, and wickedly clever. He's Kin, of the Sun, and his power over heat and light comes from the Sun. He has connections everywhere, including with Dagon, and has run afoul of The Association. He's married to Natural Scott, and will happily punch anybody who has a problem with that.

**The Throne:** One of the two ancient magical items which control the world of the Fey by siphoning all Fey magic (and some non-Fey from the Stolen). The power they wield goes beyond comprehension, and they do not share enough magic to keep their people fully well. Created after the First War by Mab, leader of the Unseelie Fey, the Throne still carries Mab's soul inside it, and sanity is... at a premium. At least it isn't the Scepter, which has a tendency to destroy its chosen ruler after a time.

# TERMS

**The Association:** An organization dedicated to the preservation of humanity in the face of genetic extinction. They hold humanity as the pinnacle of evolution, and view the magic-using Mythos as a horrific mutation. Their goal is to exterminate these creatures and "save" the human race.

**Fey Portal:** Fey magical doorways through the Void, accessed through a specific item like a coin or knife or book. While the power to use one must be secured in the item beforehand, anyone capable of using one can travel anywhere they wish to go. There are a lot of questions about these portals. Often, they come with a heavy sense of being watched, and not by friendly eyes...

**Feyling:** A child Fey. Gender isn't really considered pre-puberty, so this word is neutral.

**Grey:** Fey who have been cut off from The Scepter and The Throne as an ultimate form of punishment. It means slow starvation of self or of pride, because grey Fey must find other ways to gather magic (some say *steal*) and keep themselves alive.

**New Delhi Incident**: A world-shattering event taking place during *Half-Blood Prophecies* that revealed the magical Mythos to the Ever-Dying world. The Red and Black dragon clans broke into warfare, and their battle spilled into the night sky, in full view of everyone—and New Delhi being one of the premier cities for technology in the world, it quickly became impossible to erase or ruin the amount of surveillance. It was impossible to ignore that dragons were real, and (leery of panicking humans seeking out and attacking lone members of the Mythos) the Fey made the choice to come forward, presenting an attractive, human-like representative for the Ever-Dying nations to make peace with.

**Night-Child**: The source of all "vampire" rumors, Night-Children are an ancient and frightening breed, and very difficult to kill. They must be made from humans; with only a few exceptions, any magic in the blood prevents transformation. Once they are *made*, transformed into something far different from human, several key details remain: one, no matter ethnic heritage, all of them have the same green eyes, which have a tendency to glow. Two, they all carry a hunger they call the Beast—a mad bloodlust, which, if ignored, drives the Night-Child insane. They must drink human blood, though it does not need to be to the death. Three, they all inherit an ability they call *going to dust*. It's called "dust" because that's what it looks like—dust motes swirling in sunlight. It isn't dust, however. It's impossible to retain, control, or stop; it can pass through any solid surface, and travel at unbelievable speeds. No one fully understands how this works. Notte controls his family strictly. Ravena, not so much, though even they may not cross certain lines.

**Umbra:** The home of the Darkness. It doesn't have light in the sense we understand it, and without special magical application, one cannot see there at all.

**Void:** The strange space through which Fey portals travel. All that anybody really knows is that's where the gods live, and it is... not a safe place.

*Want more? There is a full wiki on <u>https://ruthannereid.com/</u>. Enjoy!*

# NO ONE WRITES ALONE

This particular novella comes on the heels of discovering an incredible community: the fans and creator of *Malevolent*, the horror podcast. Harlan, you're an inspiration, straight-up. I threw Jack in here as an homage (though I somehow doubt he's as you pictured him). I tossed the names Lester, Yang, and Doe in as an extra shout-out, and I highly encourage anyone who enjoys character-driven cosmic horror to check *Malevolent* out.

And as for the members of the Gearsussy Discord server: you are my joy, my cheering section, and my partners in crime. The other names of the nine Kin families are references to their original characters: Josef Roth, from Charlie; June Williams, from Flamia; and Odd (the) Bard, from Kraiva. (Sims and Blackwood are just because I am and always will be a *Magnus Archives* fan, but that's a whole other story.)

And as always, my husband provided the best feedback, encouragement, and needful reminders to rest. I love you, Duane.

# ABOUT THE AUTHOR

A bestselling author, Ruthanne Reid has led panels on world-building, taught courses on plot and character development, and been the keynote speaker for the Write Practice Retreat. Author of nine books and dozens of short stories, she makes daily videos to help other creatives get unblocked and into a healthy habit of creation.

Ruthanne has lived in her head since childhood, when she used up her mom's red typewriter ribbon writing a story about a pony princess and a genocidal snake-kingdom. When she isn't reading, writing, or reading about writing, Ruthanne enjoys old cartoons with her husband and cats, and dreams of living on an island far, far away.

Find her on: https://youtube.com/ruthannereid | https://patreon.com/ruthannereid/ | https://ruthannereid.com/